Luz Marina doesn't quite fit the ı
ingénue, but the initial impression she gives is of a
young woman endearing in her innocence.

The sultry South American beauty is naïve, or perhaps
ambitious enough, to have her head turned by the
notorious Jose Maria Serrano, a main player in the
illicit Colombian drugs trade.

Their liaison, which starts with a declaration of " te
amo," at the Teatro in Bogota, is under pressure from
the very start. The fairytale soon begins to deconstruct
when bit by bit it starts to dawn on Luz Marina that she
has not, after all, married the man of her dreams.

Will their marriage last "hasta que la muerte nos
separe?"

Ironically it will be in the hills, lochs and glens of far-
away romantic Scotland that she will eventually learn
the truth – but not immediately, and certainly not
before many other innocent people, including the
Hunter family from Inverness, and the redoubtable
Detective Superintendent Iain Ramsay and his team,

are drawn into the web and intrigues of the charismatic Serrano.

Jose Maria's lieutenant and bodyguard, Paulo, has been with him since they were both boys in the back streets of Bucaramanga.

Serrano trusts no one in the whole world but Paulo.

(((((Shockwave)))))

Debut Novel by Dawson Lamont

ISBN 9781787233058

Copyright © Dawson Lamont 2018

First Publication in Great Britain

-Chapter One-

Somewhere northwest of Milarrochy Bay on Loch Lomond is a sandbank that now has a special meaning for the Hunters. They are just your average family from the beautiful Scottish Highlands - Mum, Dad and two sons. But far away, thousands of miles away in Colombia and as far removed from their idyllic lives as one can possibly get, Jose Maria Serrano - possibly the shrewdest drugs baron in modern times since Pablo Escobar - was doing something that would send a real shockwave through their world.

The boys had arrived at the loch one Saturday morning in May. They had towed their sports boat, a Bayliner, by car all the way from a small village near Stirling, where it was stored for most of the year on its road trailer in a secure parking compound.

The journey had been uneventful with David's elderly but treasured Jaguar saloon just managing to cope with the bumps, twists and turns of the A811 as it crosses the country between Stirling and Balloch; a journey punctuated by pit stops to quench the considerable thirst of the old lady, not to mention the beer demands of the intermittently mutinous young crew.

From the very early days, Ollie as she was affectionately to be known had been a glint in her future Captain's eye. It was one day in 2010 as David Hunter had toured the stands at the Scottish Outdoor Leisure Exhibition in Glasgow that he began to realise owning such a boat could become a reality. What better way was there, after all, for a landlubber and his two sons to indulge a childhood fantasy than to become master of one's own vessel, "sailing the seven seas" and venturing into places that those of a more pedestrian persuasion would never see?

He had rehearsed in his mind all the positive aspects of uncharacteristically throwing caution to the wind and putting his hard-earned money where his mouth was.

There was the "fresh air" argument – most convincing with the boat imagined at full tilt and the exhaust from the 3-litre MerCruiser being lost in the glorious 45mph wake generated off the stern;

the "family" justification – it provided an extra reason to visit and spend time with his children; and the "better than a motorbike" reasoning, whereby he could recapture his lost youth and expand his personal horizons without risking his neck astride the latest flash BMW tourer on the most dangerous road in the country, the A9 that led to his home town of Inverness.

When a later search of the Internet revealed a new boat complete with a road trailer being offered for sale at a discount of fifteen per cent and identical to the one on show in the Glasgow exhibition, the die was cast. It mattered not that he had little powerboat experience, the seller was in Northern Ireland, or that collecting his new toy would mean a round trip by road and sea of some 600 miles. They were meant for each other.

And so by this innocent purchase, began an adventure that would span the world, bringing family upheaval and exposure to dangers beyond David's imagining.

-Chapter Two-

For those familiar with the Duncan MacKinnon Memorial Slipway at Balloch on Loch Lomond, this is an excellent facility allowing even the most inexperienced of boaters the opportunity to safely launch and retrieve their craft, and to enjoy the iconic delights of the loch.

Not that the Hunters needed the help that was on offer from National Park employees that morning. With a full season now under their belts they were old hands at the game and swiftly made Ollie shipshape and Bristol-fashion. Even the skipper had mastered the task of delicately reversing his pride and joy safely down the launching ramp without extreme zigzagging – no mean feat when the overall length of the ensemble is almost 40 feet, and the boat is of independent mind.

For a modern craft assembled in Mexico and with a hull design that would shame many a NASA engineer, she fitted surprisingly well into the "picture postcard" that was the Loch. Even the Maid of the Loch herself seemed to approve, as she looked down on her younger sister afloat at the adjacent pontoon.

David had his usual family crew of Rory and Stuart with him that day and they went meticulously through their "pre-flight" preparations such as "Is the bung in?" and "Are the hoses all connected?" before donning their mandatory lifejackets and awakening the Mercruiser beast. The captain was at the helm as usual, with the safety kill-cord carefully attached to his wrist as they left the 11 kilometres per hour speed restriction zone and he gradually opened the throttle.

Very soon the trim of the sterndrive was raised and Ollie rose obligingly to the plane. In no time at all the bowrider was skimming effortlessly from wave to wave while lesser vessels wallowed in the troughs.

A powerful wake now streaked out behind her, at least as impressive in relative terms as the trail from the two Rolls-Royce RB211 turbofans of a far away Boeing 757 in the blue sky above.

In the nearer distance a seaplane, an amphibious Cessna 208, taxied gently out from the jetty at Cameron House Hotel across the loch. As the plane took off, the well-heeled tourists on board waved down at the tiny sports boat some 100 feet below. The water sparkled in the bright spring sunshine and with the unique backdrop of rugged Ben Lomond and the heather-clad hills all was right with the world.

Unbeknown to captain and crew, however, they were the subject of intense interest from an individual on the west shore. He was observing them keenly through powerful binoculars from the comfort of a Range Rover parked next to the Duck Bay marina.

-Chapter Three-

Edward Charles Fortescue to give him his Sunday
name was a big lad. Known only as Ted to his friends
of whom there were precious few, he was better known
in Paisley as "the animal." He acted as enforcer for
several local personalities in the West of Scotland, none
of whom would ever be invited to join the local Rotary
Club. He was not from these parts, and with his East
End accent, he made no attempt to hide the fact. His
grandparents had actually hailed from Chelsea, but he
and his father before him had been the black sheep of
the family.

Most people would consider it a pleasure to sit behind
the wheel of an Evoque, but not Ted. Despite the air
conditioning he was sweating profusely as he
manoeuvred his considerable frame so that he had the
best view of his target. He hated these assignments
where an element of discretion and patience was
required. To him the use of brute force was the only

way to get results. - He had several medals from Porterfield and Barlinnie to prove it.

He had been on the road since 4am that morning and the withdrawal symptoms from overindulgence the previous day did not help. Unlike Ollie, he was not in good trim.

Just before dawn he had been crossing the Kincardine Bridge when he spotted what might have been an undercover police car taking a particular interest in his vehicle. He had managed to give them the slip, but could not risk being pulled over with dodgy plates. What could he do? He was now back in the Dunmore area, heading east with the River Forth somewhere on his left. He could see the chimneystacks of the Grangemouth refinery burning in the far distance, but had nowhere to hide.

Desperately he scanned the road in front of him.

He could not believe his good luck. There was a sign to what looked like a huge caravan park off to his right. Despite all the apparent security someone had left the gate slightly ajar; not enough for a vehicle, but sufficient for him to ease his considerable bulk through.

He left his vehicle off the road, and outside the facility among some trees, but there was still a danger of it being spotted and searched by the boys in blue. His fevered brain was working overtime.

He had a blue hoodie with him. - Not good for the street cred', but sufficient to cover his face as he squeezed through the gate and past the security camera.

With him he carried the parcel that had been entrusted to him, destined for Aberdeen and the northern supply chain.

His plan was simple. He would lie low, spending what remained of the hours of darkness in one of the several hundred touring and residential caravans stored on the site. Like a single fish amongst a shoal of sardines there should be safety in numbers. But he could not risk discovery with the package in his charge, a packet that he knew had the potential to destroy the lives of many. He would hide it separately at the furthermost end of the large site before grabbing a few hours' sleep.

Site fifty-two fitted the bill. He knew it was fifty-two because it said so in large numbers, which he could still read despite the fact that this was a dark corner of the compound. Amongst all the caravans a newish looking boat was stored on a road trailer, carefully covered in several layers of tarpaulin. It took Ted about ten minutes to gain access, do what needed to be done and creep back to take his pick of the rent-free luxury caravans.

He was woken rudely from his fitful slumbers about 8am, disturbed by the noise of a vehicle crossing the gravel in front of his comfortable van. He was troubled by his predicament. He had seen what happened to fellow couriers who had messed up. - It was not pretty.

He lumbered to the window of his squat, just in time to see a blue Jaguar X-Type exiting the yard. There was nothing unusual about that, but what followed the car almost precipitated a heart attack, and certainly a need for clean boxers! - It was an elegant sports boat, now minus the blue tarpaulins and bearing the registration number LL9615.

-Chapter Four-

By way of contrast, the Hunters had been up bright and early and en route for Balloch in excellent spirits. They had hitched up their boat to the Jaguar in record time. Within 20 minutes they were heading west, complete with picnic hamper, waterskiis and other paraphernalia.

They had fuelled up at a Stirling service station just off the M90, convenient for car and boat to access the pumps but expensive fuel for a day on the water, and began to make their way across to the west. Both crew members snoozed for the first half hour or so, wakening up only to criticise some aspect, often imaginary, of the skipper's driving; or to make their vital beer and crisps selection for later in the day.

The beer stop, by now a longstanding family tradition was at a village called Buchlyvie, about 15 miles from Loch Lomond. This stop was chosen because it was possible to park the "Jagollie" ensemble opposite the off-licence with relative ease and, importantly, without disrupting the traffic flow on what was quite a narrow road.

At that time the roads were relatively quiet, so they were soon bowling along, looking forward to an exciting day on the water.

Just how exciting they were not to know…

Back in Dunmore, Ted who had slept in his clothes and who by now would have been the easiest of targets for the dumbest of police sniffer dogs, flung his large frame through the narrow caravan door and bolted for the exit. By this time another vehicle was leaving the compound, and he had the good fortune to be able to clamber quietly on to its open trailer out of view of the solitary driver. By so doing he avoided the security gates and the camera. These, he presumed correctly, were now operating normally. Once outside the caravan compound and again wearing his hood, he jumped down, made his way across the field and through the trees to where he had abandoned the stolen Range Rover the previous night. He was relieved to find it exactly as he had left it.

He knew that the vehicle, despite its forty thousand pounds price tag didn't really matter. If he was to save his own skin he had to retrieve only the merchandise, and fast. Nothing else mattered.

Fast wasn't something that Edward normally did. It was not for nothing that his school chums had christened him Tim rather than Ted, and this unfortunate nomenclature had stuck during his early years. Indeed psychiatrists might say this was the catalyst for him becoming a bit of a loner and entering a life of crime.

But think fast he must. "Where could one take a sports boat within easy reach of the Stirling area? Would they go east to the near-at-hand Forth, south to the Clyde coast, or west to whatever lay beyond?" Ted hadn't excelled in geography at school, so he really didn't have a clue.

And then, as he sat at the wheel with head in hands the blindingly obvious came to him in a flash.

He remembered the boat's registration number, or at least the letters that prefixed it. "LL" could only mean one thing. - He programmed Loch Leven into the vehicle's SatNav and set off confidently in an easterly direction.

After about five miles, he was rounding a bend when he could not help but notice a large billboard advertising lodges in a picturesque lochside location. He had driven well past this before his neural pathways connected and he went back for a second look. Of course, it was Loch Lomond! How could he have been so stupid?

With an expletive worthy of his calling as "the animal," he entered the postcode from the billboard into his SatNav, and did a lightning U-turn that sprayed gravel from the vehicle's wheels all over the road. This put the Fear of God into a couple of elderly lady motorists in an oncoming Mini, but by this time Ted had disappeared at high speed around the next bend - leaving them, sadly, with palpitations and at the very least a need for a partial vehicle respray.

What you can't do of course, in Central Scotland, is drive a conspicuous vehicle with blacked-out windows at breakneck speed on rural roads without attracting a modicum of attention from fellow motorists. By the time Ted reached the village of Cambusbarron he had realised this and moderated his speed a little. He was confident that he would eventually catch up with his quarry, even if it meant some unwanted travel in the meantime.

-Chapter Five-

As they drew out of Buchlyvie, the boys noticed the four-by-four that recklessly overtook them on a dangerous bend. Reference was made to the parentage of the driver. Little did they know how true this was. Neither did they realise that he had pulled off the road into some bushes at a layby near Gartocharn, waiting for them to pass so that he could tail them all the way to their destination.

Ted for his part was not enjoying the journey. The road to Balloch is a narrow one, full of twists and turns and some potholes to trap the unwary. He was used to motorway travel and being able to overtake when he chose to do so. Instead he was hemmed in most of the way behind a Tesco lorry and a foreign tourist who was driving a hired Fiat Punto. Just fast enough to prevent anyone overtaking, but slowly and erratically enough to remind Ted why he himself had been recommended several times for anger management classes.

Unfortunately for our hero, the fact that his Range Rover had one hundred and seventy-eight horses under the bonnet was of little consequence in these circumstances, whereas the less powerful Jag at the head of the traffic, and with an experienced driver who knew the road inside out, had a clear towing run all the way to the lochside. When David turned right at one of several junctions en route, the hot and bothered Ted failed to notice and carried straight on towards Glasgow behind the Punto.

That was why it took him a full two hours to eventually reach the far shore of Loch Lomond and find himself on the road to Luss. He knew there must be an access to the loch off the Luss Road because he had seen the marina signposted.

"Perhaps that would be where his quarry had been heading?"

But Loch Lomond is a big expanse of water, 24 miles long to be exact, with a width of between 0.75 miles and 5 miles. Ted had parked as close as he could to the water's edge, but he might as well have slept on in his caravan squat that morning. To him the task seemed futile. Then, when rummaging later for his i-Phone, he spotted the high-powered binoculars in the furthermost recesses of the glove box and couldn't believe his luck.

He had a reasonable vantage point, from which he could see straight across to Balloch. To his left were the magnificent heather-clad hills below the mighty Ben Lomond, all of 3,195 feet high. To his right was the end of the loch and the commercial development that houses the Lomond Shores Shopping Centre.

In the distance he could see the old Maid of the Loch steamer resplendent in her livery of red, white and black; still a tourist icon, but now a sad relic of past glories – a bit like the Royal Yacht Britannia in Leith, or even worse the Queen Elizabeth 2, laid up in Port Rashid since June 2009, still awaiting conversion to the floating luxury hotel beside the Palm Jumeirah that had been promised by Istithmar, the private equity arm of Dubai World.

Ted had seen the QE2 once when carrying out enforcement duties in the Middle East but had been in no fit state to remember much about it. His was a high adrenalin career, and his singular focus meant he had no time for the finer things in life.

It was now approaching midday. Ollie and her crew had enjoyed an exhilarating morning on the water, practising some safety manoeuvres and their boat handling techniques, even gingerly exploring the inner reaches of the River Leven as it runs through the town of Balloch; but mostly enjoying the fresh air and camaraderie that comes with a breath-taking Scottish location and the bottles of fine local brew that as every mariner knows are essential ballast on board. There was usually bubby for any ladies present but today was an exception, a Boys' Day Out.

"Let's water ski to the pub on Inchmurrin" said Stuart. "I am sure that they'll be serving bar lunches on the island by now, and I am a bit peckish."

"Why not?" said Rory, "I could murder a beer."

Within a few minutes distinctive "Spiderman" wetsuits were donned, and the captain (outvoted as usual when he had suggested a spot of fishing as an alternative to skiing or wakeboarding) was soon back at the helm, speeding in a north-easterly direction as his crew skied expertly on the waves behind.

Ten minutes later the Hunters were level with Duck Bay Marina and although at some distance, the blue Bayliner entered clearly into Ted Fortescue's field of vision.

-Chapter Six-

The enforcer hated being confined. It probably had
something to do with his spells of incarceration at Her
Majesty's pleasure. He would have given up his long
surveillance some considerable time ago if his very life
hadn't depended upon the outcome. That was no
exaggeration. So he had to sit and sweat in the heat of
the vehicle.

He knew from the tabloid press that recent research has
shown one particular gene type to be more susceptible
to excessive perspiration than the rest, but why did his
DNA have to be affected in this way? He was in denial
that his diet and alcohol consumption had anything at
all to do with his current condition. He remained
convinced that alcohol's effects were wholly beneficial,
and directly proportional to units consumed.

The air conditioning was switched on from time to
time, but he had to conserve his fuel for operational
activity. After all, he didn't know the geography of the
area. From what he had seen, filling stations were few

and far between. And he didn't want to leave a CCTV trail if he could avoid it. Nowadays there were cameras everywhere, even in Argyll and Bute.

He was fast sinking into depression. His life seriously would be at an end if he didn't complete his current assignment. Bigger fish than he was had received a bullet on their doorstep, or even worse a machete where it didn't belong!

He sat hunched up, a picture of misery, but still he kept the heavy binoculars to his eyes. The sweat ran down his back and he could feel it already soaking his waistband. He speculated as to his fate. Only several weeks before an acquaintance of Fortescue from Saltcoats (he had no real friends) had been found "deep drowned in Doon."

Several long hours passed.

At first he thought it was a mirage. It seemed hot enough for one in the stuffy environment of the car, and he had seen many a strange sight in the Persian Gulf. He rubbed his red eyes in disbelief and then with some difficulty carefully retrained his binoculars upon the loch. But yes, he really had found his elusive target!

With one bound, Ted was out of the vehicle and running down the steep slippery steps to the jetty.

-Chapter Seven-

James Brown felt only a thump to his back, and saw
and heard nothing more.

A gentle soul, an inveterate Glasgow Rangers supporter
before the Club's unfortunate departure from the
Scottish Premier League in 2012, he used to live by
himself in the shadow of Ibrox Stadium. With his
friendly banter and penchant for Tunnock's teacakes,
he was a particular favourite of the Park Rangers who
regularly patrol the loch.

He frequently went out alone on the water, usually to
fish and the patrols in their fast RIBs kept an eye open
for him. Today was to be no exception.

His family had been warning him for years about his
solo boating trips, always having his lifejacket on
board, but seldom wearing it.

As fate would have it he never even reached the boat.
His head struck a rock as he fell from the steps. As the

autopsy later showed, he had no chance of survival in the water although it was only some 4 feet deep at that point, and at 5 degrees relatively warm by Scottish standards.

"Problem solved," thought Ted as he leapt callously over his victim into the freshly fuelled cabin cruiser, with its engine already conveniently running.

He had no experience of boats, but sure as hell that wasn't going to deter him from catching up with the blue and white Bayliner, now in the far distance but at least within his sight. From what he could see there was still at least one skier following the boat, so he was confident that he would be alongside soon.

He scarcely had given any thought to what he would do when the moment of rendezvous arrived, just as he gave no thought to the poor innocent that he had so callously murdered at the jetty.

"A simple accident and nothing more" would be the likely verdict, he thought.

And so the chase was on.

-Chapter Eight-

The Hunters, quite oblivious to matters on the west shore, had thoroughly enjoyed a couple of hours' water skiing on the unusually mirror-like surface. They were now drying themselves off in the warm sun. Music from a local radio station, Heart FM, provided distraction from the fearsome roar of the engine.

It was a leisurely run of only fifteen minutes to the island of Inchmurrin (named after Saint Mirin, like the Paisley football team), where they could tie up at the convenient jetty and go ashore as planned for a well-earned pint in the solitary local hostelry.

Inchmurrin happens to be the largest fresh water island in the British Isles and together with Creinch, Torrinch and Inchcailloch forms part of the Highland boundary fault. It has an interesting history going back over many centuries and was used by the aristocracy for hunting at least as far back as the early 14th century. King Robert 1 of Scotland even had a hunting lodge built there and established a deer park. Later, in 1617 when James V1 made his only return visit to Scotland he insisted upon including hunting on Inchmurrin in his itinerary.

At various times the island has been the site of a 7th Century monastery, been raided by Rob Roy, seen several murders of the Colquhouns of Luss, been used as a mental asylum, and curiously been recognised as a remote enough secret location for unmarried pregnant women to go to, to give birth.

In more recent years the island has played host to some extremely hardy naturists (although much to the boys' disappointment, none had ever been encountered by the Hunters), been used for weddings and had even provided the venue for haggis hurling competitions. A World Record throw of a haggis (weighing one pound eight ounces, after plucking) - of 180 feet 10 inches was set at Inchmurrin in August 1984, and lasted for a remarkable 20 years.

The Hunter boys had heard all these stories from David before. He could be very convincing, however implausible the subject matter; after all he had spent most of his career in the public sector. On this occasion, the details were again true, as Rory had confirmed the facts on Wikipedia!

As as an alternative to visiting his favourite island again, they wondered if they should push on up the loch to Balmaha.

The crew were noisily debating the merits of these options when all at once they were rudely interrupted.

Suddenly, out of the corner of his eye, the skipper had caught sight of another boat approaching really fast from astern. He hadn't heard her at all.

The yellow buoys off Inchmurrin meant that they were now within another 11 kilometres per hour speed-restriction zone but it soon became apparent that the other, larger vessel was on a collision course with Ollie, closing very fast and seemingly out of control.

Drastic action was required.

Rory had been standing up at that moment in the bow area. When the skipper opened the throttle wide and let loose all 135 horsepower, his crewmember had no chance of retaining his balance. He fell heavily into the centre of the boat. Thankfully he managed to remain on board. He was already hurling abuse at the helmsman when he too spotted the danger from astern.

He also felt the rush of a small calibre bullet as it passed over his head. This was no warning shot across their bows. Falling when he did had undoubtedly saved his life! He thought better of continuing his rant at the skipper.

Unless faced with such danger it is difficult to forecast one's reactions.

The crew responded in the only way possible that day. They kept their heads down as several more bullets whistled overhead. None of them had ever heard a gun fired in earnest. In truth they were semi-paralysed with fear, but tried desperately to outrun the pirate. All their bravado had fast disappeared.

"Was this really happening? This was Loch Lomond, in the West of Scotland where the locals were famed worldwide for their friendly disposition and hospitable nature."

Feverishly the captain veered this way and that, at the same time trying to put some space between the two vessels. He was succeeding, only just, but they would be safe only for as long as Ted's gun was kept in its shoulder holster.

In the Bayliner 175GT, the fuel tank is located aft, beside the engine. It contains unleaded petrol.

The potential for disaster was enormous.

-Chapter Nine-

It is not easy to steer a fast boat with one hand while you are lying on your front on a hard GRP floor between the front seats. This, however, was what had to be done. The helmsman had zero visibility. He already had a stiff neck from straining to see the compass. It was above him and to the left of the helm.

Against his better judgement David had been forced to ditch the ignition "kill cord," which did not quite reach to his unorthodox helmsman's position and all he could really do was steer what he hoped was a straight course, and pray. The engine revs were in the red zone, and so was his blood pressure.

At one point they very nearly collided with the local waterbus, plying its daily trade from the mainland to several of the smaller islands. She was steering in a southwesterly direction and passed at very close range between Ollie and her pursuer.

There was palpable fear etched on the faces of the twenty or so waterbus passengers when their vessel was caught in the considerable wakes of the two boats travelling at excessive speed.

Had the passengers known the reality of the situation, they would not have believed it. As it was, some of them wondered briefly why the sports boat appeared to be unmanned. It was only as they came closer that they realised that the passengers were lying down. "How strange was that!"

The moment passed however. When the second wake hit the waterbus and it rolled alarmingly from port to starboard and back again, they were all far too busy holding on to each other and to their seats, to worry about it further. One unfortunate American in a garish shirt and voluminous shorts later said that the experience was "awesome," but he still had lost his expensive camera with all his holiday photographs over the side.

By this time Stuart, who was lying awkwardly across the rear of the Bayliner cabin and soaked through by the spray, had the presence of mind to reach for his mobile phone to alert the authorities. He dialled 999. He was about to be connected when with impeccable timing the boat jolted and the phone disappeared from his wet hand into the far depths of the engine compartment. Oh, how the crew wished that their penny-pinching skipper had taken up the option of installing a fixed VHF radio!

The day's gentle recreation that they had been looking forward to for so long was not going at all according to plan.

-Chapter Ten-

Ted was concerned that his target was fast disappearing. He was desperately agitated, his face even more beetroot-red than usual.

He had worked out eventually that there was no way that his larger and heavier boat could compete with the Bayliner's raw power and superior power-to-weight ratio.

He had tried throwing some of the cruiser's kit and furniture overboard in order to lessen the weight, and even the heavy anchor and chain that he had only remembered to unfasten from the bow and from his person at the very last moment, but to no avail.

He once again raised his gun, aimed directly for the stern of Ollie and pulled the trigger.

At the same time the skipper was considering his options. His immediate concern was that the 21-gallon fuel tank gauge was reading less than one tenth full. At his current speed fuel was probably being consumed at the rate of 4 miles per gallon, so they had a very limited range. Less than 10 miles, he reckoned. On the other hand, he was managing to outrun the larger vessel. And so he had little choice but to press on.

As soon as Ted pulled the trigger he knew that something was wrong. His gun had not fired. He had had his six. He watched in fury as Ollie gradually disappeared into the distance.

David and the boys by this time were desperately uncomfortable with having to lie down bouncing about on the hard cockpit floor. They gingerly raised their heads above the transom; a bit like infantrymen from the trenches in World War One. They reckoned that the vessel chasing them must already be out of range, so they consulted their chart and started to plan their escape route. A decent chart plotter would have come in handy, but theirs did not provide the necessary level of detail for inland waters. Fortunately, however, the skipper had a reasonable knowledge of navigating the loch.

They would proceed in their current direction and attempt to lose their pursuer amongst some of the smaller islands. This would then give them time to turn off the engine and retrieve the lost mobile phone from the engine bay.

The nearest point at which they could contact the authorities was probably Inchfad or Millarochy Bay, but anywhere would do. They needed to reach shore, abandon Ollie and make themselves scarce as soon as possible.

With a degree of reality returning to the situation, David felt confident enough to raise the engine cowling, with a view to seeing if he could find the lost phone.

When he did so, his heart almost missed a beat. There were several inches of water, at least six he thought, in the normally dry engine compartment. The level appeared to be rising. Subconsciously he had thought that Ollie was a bit heavy in the water, but he had never thought to check the bilges. That would have been impossible anyway with all of them lying on the floor.

With the electric bilge pump soon deployed, they made as fast as they could for the nearest island, which happened to be Inchboggin. Five minutes into the passage he checked the bilge again. It was still at least as full as before. Even when Rory set to work furiously with a manual pump and Stuart with a yellow plastic bailer, the water refused to go down. One of the gunman's shots must have done some damage and they were in a bit of a predicament!

A frantic check of the engine bay failed to find the mobile phone, but the water slopping about down there would probably have ruined it anyway.

Loch Lomond is well provided with pontoons for mooring leisure craft. But like the proverbial London omnibus, there is never one when or where you need it most. David knew this, and that this island, like many on the loch, was uninhabited. Nevertheless he headed fast for the nearest shingle. Terra firma was his immediate priority if they were not to end up swimming. His normal caution of keeping a weather eye on the depth gauge was thrown to the wind.

With a severe jolt Ollie hit a sandbank about 20 yards from shore, and almost instantaneously the high performance aluminium prop smashed on a rock that was barely visible in the peaty water.

The Hunters had no time to consider why a crazed gunman was on their tail. Whether they liked it or not, that was the reality of their predicament.

They prepared immediately to abandon ship.

But they were to have their answer. David hardly had one foot in the water when an innocuous parcel wrapped in soggy brown paper floated up to meet him from the bilges below. It clearly belonged to someone else. It looked like they wanted it back. At any cost!

It was the answer, but it certainly wasn't the one they wanted.

-Chapter Eleven-

Crime and despair are strange bedfellows. Ted knew them both well. Usually the despair came after a sentencing for his most recent crime, either because he was not clever enough to evade capture or his well-paid solicitor was unable on the basis of the facts provided, to construct any reasonable illusion of a case in his defence. Sometimes it came when one of his many "friends" gave evidence for the prosecution.

He was used to following orders. Despair set in when all was not going according to plan -usually on those occasions when he had to think for himself. In old computer parlance, he was an operator rather than a systems analyst.

By now he was ravenously hungry and his thirst was such that he even stopped briefly and tried drinking some of the water from the loch. He had heard somewhere that Loch Lomond served as a reservoir for much of Glasgow. One sip however was enough to make him gag, so he quickly abandoned that idea.

To make matters worse, he had seen his target disappear steadily into the distance, and a feeling of complete helplessness was again overcoming him. Where could they be? Without them, it would be farewell Fortescue!

He hated boats with a vengeance. "Why were they subject to the vagaries of wind and tide? Why would they never go where you wanted them to, and why did they have no brakes?" More importantly, "why did he nearly always end up getting wet?" - The answers to these and many more mysteries were beyond him.

He sat in the wheelhouse and once again pondered the unfairness of life. In consolation he stole more than a few slugs of The Macallan whisky from the bottle kindly left in the galley area by the late James Brown.

Eventually, he decided to turn around and search in a different direction. He would do so for as long as it was daylight and he had fuel in the tank. Despite there being no method in this, no organised search plan whatsoever for over 20 miles of unfamiliar loch, he had to keep going. Mile after dreary mile.

Half an hour passed, then an hour, then two.

Just when he thought that all hope had gone, he rounded a headland and was astonished to spot the abandoned Bayliner, some 100 meters ahead. He drove straight for it, throwing his vessel into reverse as he approached, but his reactions were impaired. He did not slow down sufficiently to avoid damaging both boats quite badly in the process.

Ted picked himself up wearily from where he had fallen from the helmsman's seat, grazing his shin in the process, and cursing as only he could.

He pulled himself together and even before he clumsily boarded the hastily abandoned Ollie, he had spotted the brown paper parcel lying conspicuously in the bow area.

Only then did he begin to breathe a little more normally.

-Chapter Twelve-

David, Rory and Stuart had reached the highest point of the island. They had abandoned all their belongings and waded frantically through the shallow water without even removing their shoes. Once ashore they made their way through the deep undergrowth to the rudimentary path that leads across the island. David, fortunately, had some knowledge of his whereabouts since on a previous trip he had picnicked on the island. He seemed to remember a boathouse on the north side.

It had been Rory's idea to leave the package of drugs in a prominent location on Ollie. It was his fervent hope that their pursuer would settle for their recovery and abandon the chase.

But they were not taking any chances. Even crack SAS-trained personnel being pursued by terrorists could not have made their way more stealthily up the hill. Every so often they would stop, crouch down in the bracken and listen intently, aware that their every movement or snapped twig might be heard from down below.

From the clearing at the summit they had a clear view back to the far side of the bay in which Ollie had been left. So they knew that a cabin cruiser had followed them in. If they were in any doubt as to the identity of the craft, they could not fail to hear the roar of its engine in reverse and the expensive bang of the subsequent collision.

Blind panic made them race down the slippery path on the north side, paying scant heed to National Park exhortations to protect the natural environment of Loch Lomond. Several wild orchids and other horticultural specimens suffered underfoot, but the tiny purple plants weren't even seen by the trio as they crashed breathlessly through the undergrowth.

They hadn't waited long enough at the top to see if their pursuer had left the island or not. They scarcely had time to draw breath. They could not afford to take any chances.

Soon the boathouse was in sight.

Stuart prised open the side door with a rusty old hinge that he found lying on the path. He peered through the gloom. It seemed at first that the boathouse was empty. Suddenly, however, they heard the sound of a man's voice close behind them. Rory and Stuart froze rigid on the spot.

"You'll have had your tea?"

David had recognised the boatman's voice. It was Hamish Mackenzie, originally from Auld Reekie, but now from Balloch. He sighed with immense relief. The spontaneous manhug that poor old Hamish received from David was so friendly that the elderly gentleman was left in a state of severe shock.

Before long David had contacted the Loch Patrol boat on Hamish's VHF radio and a full police search for the gunman was taking place. As the sun began to sink slowly in the west, there were all the signs of intense police activity, especially at Duck Bay Marina. A Strathclyde police chopper was also visible scouring the loch.

Although the boys in blue didn't yet know it, Ted had scuttled the stolen cabin cruiser in 60 feet of water shortly after retrieving his merchandise from Ollie. He was already making his way over to Balmaha on the east shore, courtesy of the Avon inflatable and outboard engine that the ill-fated James Brown had put together on deck in preparation for his intended fishing trip.

As reported on the television news that night,

"The shaken crew of a Bayliner sports boat who suffered a prolonged and apparently unprovoked gun attack by an as yet unnamed individual, were swiftly transferred to the mainland for medical checks and to be interviewed by the police while their vessel, which had sustained two bullet holes was patched up, towed to the National Park slipway at Milarrochy Bay and impounded as part of the evidence gathering process. A police investigation is underway to see if there is any connection with a body of an adult male found earlier in the water at Duck Bay."

It would, in fact, be well over a year before Ollie would be released back to David Hunter, but his only concern that day was that his crewmen were unharmed.

Just at that moment he never wanted to see a boat again.

-Chapter Thirteen-

From his vantage point in a hired police helicopter high above the loch, Detective Superintendent Iain Ramsay was in charge of Operation Duck Bay.

It was early in the afternoon when a member of the public walking his dog had spotted what looked like a body next to a pontoon at the marina. Initial indications were that the victim had slipped, been knocked unconscious in the fall and subsequently drowned. He was not a pretty sight but, although rare, such assumed accidents were not unknown on Scotland's favourite recreational loch.

Since then the incident had been upgraded. The helicopter had been scrambled at 4pm. Additional factors had come to light that put an entirely different complexion upon matters.

Firstly, there was a report to the local marina office of a cabin cruiser being driven erratically. It was soon established through a telephone conversation with the National Park staff at Drumkinnon Bay that the vessel in question, which was registered with them, belonged to the deceased.

"Was theft the motive?"

Secondly a Mr Swilley, waterbus operator for the Luss to Balmaha route, had filed a complaint about 2pm with the Loch Patrol about boats travelling at excessive speed within the 11kph restricted zone.

Worryingly, there were also unconfirmed reports of gunshots being heard across the loch by a concerned family having a barbeque on the beach at the north end of Inchmurrin.

Iain Ramsay still did not yet appreciate the scale of the criminal activity that he was investigating. With budgets being so tight and so many forms having to be filled in to satisfy the Force's bureaucracy, he had been reluctant to call out the chopper; but when the substance of David Hunter's call was relayed to him, he was soon in the picture.

It looked already as if one murder had been perpetrated. The search was on for those responsible. His priority was to apprehend them before anyone else got hurt.

The picture developing so far was a difficult one for DS Ramsay. He had precious few clues yet as to the circumstances surrounding the crime. He was expending resources on aerial surveillance without any guarantee of success and his cohorts on the ground were already becoming restless at the lack of direction from him. Were members of the public still at risk?

He had no murder weapon, no eyewitnesses, no forensics to speak of, and the stolen cabin cruiser appeared to have disappeared off the face of the earth. His officers were, however, methodically checking everyone and everything in the vicinity of Duck Bay, so it must surely be only a matter of time before they had some clues.

Nevertheless, as he returned from yet another sweep of the loch to his temporary incident room at the marina, Ramsay was feeling far from confident. His only consolation was that he had secured one of the craft involved. Even now ballistics experts were on their way to examine a single round that had lodged itself under the fuel tank.

The Press were already speculating as to what all the activity was about. Word had got out fast that there was a body involved.

"Was it murder?"

As Detective Superintendent Ramsay made his way through to the busy dining room of the marina complex for an impromptu press conference, it seemed that the eyes of the world were upon him.

A Sky television crew happened to have been staying in the hotel, while filming a documentary about the effect of tourism damaging the natural environment. The presence of a live news camera and sudden interest in his case made Ramsay choose his words even more carefully than usual.

-Chapter Fourteen-

At roughly the same time, Edward Charles Fortescue was polishing off a second fish supper as he walked down the main street in Alexandria. For someone with remnants of aristocratic blood flowing in his veins his manners were deplorable. His lack of social graces was appreciated, however, by the local herring gulls.

Once he had made landfall somewhere south of Balmaha he made his way inland on foot, seeking to put as much distance as he could between himself and the loch. He had been careful to sink the outboard engine 20 yards offshore and paddle in the rest of the way. Ted then proceeded with the hunting knife that he always carried about his person, to puncture and bury the Avon inflatable in a disused churchyard, before lumbering along in his inimitable style.

When he spotted a pedal cycle chained to a nearby fence post, he made short work of the padlock and proceeded smugly on his way. His considerable bulk was the ultimate challenge to the bicycle maker's engineering skills, and once again he was sweating profusely as he traversed the rough country paths.

He even managed to smile graciously at a couple of attractive girl backpackers who held open a farm gate for him as he sped on his way. The young ladies in their twenties were dressed only in crop tops and were wearing very tight shorts, but Ted's mind was elsewhere. What the girls, on holiday from Italy thought about the red haired and obese cyclist is a matter for speculation.

Perhaps they saw him as fine specimen of the typical Scottish Male, but perhaps not? - Their giggling betrayed their true feelings, as Ted's impressive rump disappeared from view.

He was congratulating himself on a job well done. He had evaded the cops, destroyed any evidence that would lead to his identification and as far as he knew, no one apart from the girls had seen his face – not even those that he had been pursuing for most of the day. Most importantly he had retrieved the merchandise, which although soggy was safely stowed in the carrier bag that contained the remains of his piscatorial repast.

In the euphoria of the moment, what he didn't realise was that his Range Rover had been the first vehicle at Duck Bay to be checked over by the uniform branch. It was now on the back of a low loader en route for central Glasgow and the closest examination known to forensic science. All CCTV cameras on routes leading to the loch were also being checked for the presence of the distinctive vehicle, and if possible an image of the occupant or occupants.

Division had alerted the drugs squad. They were already considering a list of possible suspects, several of them known to be active in low level distribution.

-Chapter Fifteen-

Two days later, Ted was barely recognisable. He had dyed his hair red and shaved off his moustache.

He had also visited a branch of Slater's Menswear in Inverness and spent 20 crisp new £20 notes on a two-piece charcoal-grey Daks suit and accessories, quite a contrast to his usual jeans and t-shirt.

He had been instructed to change his image by his controller, a man known only to him as JG. This wasn't his real name of course but then again last week he had been JY, and JT the week before that. It was all very confusing for Ted - a bit like the ever-changing vehicle licence plates issued from Swansea by the DVLA.

Ted had met one of JG's minions in Jimmy Wolf's nightclub and handed over the merchandise as instructed in a Tesco bag. The message came to him on a Pay As You Go mobile that was immediately disposed of in a deep dark pool of the River Ness. JG took no chances.

Ted then spent the next twenty-four hours hanging about the bars and restaurants of the Highland city, waiting for a further contact from JG. It never came, so he took a room in a new Premier Inn on the west side of town and laid low for a couple of days. He knew that JG was a busy man and would contact him when he was ready. Anyway, he could do with a rest.

He had never been in the City of Inverness before, and was impressed by how cosmopolitan the place was. There was a constant coming and going of tourists and business people, which meant that local people were used to seeing strangers about town. One more respectably dressed individual would be unlikely to attract attention, or so Fortescue hoped.

By the Tuesday night, he was bored. After a couple of pizzas from a takeaway on Glenurquhart Road, he took a stroll to the nearby Caledonian Canal.

He turned left past the rugby club pitches and before long found himself on the riverside outside the splendid

Eden Court Theatre. Not being much of a patron of the dramatic arts, he was walking past when he noticed that there was a big-name comedian performing that evening. He bought a ticket on the spur of the moment (cash of course) and spent the next couple of hours laughing himself stupid.

That didn't take long. The Peroni lager that he drank in copious quantities helped, and it was just as well the performance ended when it did, otherwise our Ted might have been asked to leave. A stern looking usher, nearly as intimidating in his black Eden Court uniform as Ted himself, had already warned him twice to be quiet.

He was feeling quite mellow and still stuffing his face with popcorn, when he exited the auditorium and turned right into Bishop's Road - straight into the arms of two large Polish gentlemen who invited him in broken English to favour them with his company.

Co-incidentally, David Hunter happened to be in Beauly that day, blissfully unaware that his armed pursuer of only a few days ago was no more than 15 miles away. As it happens, he could have walked past the drugs courier in the street without knowing who he was.

David sincerely hoped that the converse was true and that his attacker would not recognise him or know his location. He had hardly managed one full night's sleep since the nightmare that had been Loch Lomond.

-Chapter Sixteen-

For a seemingly douce Highland town, the fast expanding "City of Inverness" as it has been known since the Queen elevated it at the turn of the Millennium, retains a hard side that would surprise many a visitor. It is not in the same league as places in the West of Scotland like Paisley or Kilwinning, but its citizens no longer have the protection afforded by its relative geographical isolation.

With the prospect of a national Police Force for Scotland on the not too distant horizon, some consideration was even being given to routinely arming police officers as they went about their daytime and evening patrols. This wouldn't go down at all well with a majority of the local community. In the Highlands local people are loath to lock their front doors, never mind contemplate the need to have lethal force exercised in certain circumstances.

Petty criminals and those such as Fortescue posing more serious dangers to society, now have to endure no worse than a cheap fare Megabus journey of some four hours north from the central belt of Scotland before they reach the new frontier of their ambitions. The city in contrast to some of the rural areas that surround it, boasts high-speed broadband and reasonable public transport, so communications and travel are easier than they have ever been. The large influx of tourists in the summer months, together with a sizeable immigrant contingent mainly from Eastern Europe, also means that individuals can lose themselves relatively easily in Inverness and its hinterland.

Ted hoped to do that very thing. He had had no option but to come north with his latest commission for JG, but he longed to return to the relative security and pie shops of the big smoke as soon as his work was done.

His new chums from Poland were anything but friendly. Scarcely had he received their invitation, than his wrists were savagely cable-tied together and he was bundled into the rear of a Skoda parked in the Council Headquarters carpark behind Eden Court Theatre.

They drove from there westwards on the Beauly road to the remote old quarry at Cabrich near Kirkhill where they conveyed to him from his erstwhile friend JG, a "thank you message" capable of interpretation in any language. This resulted in severe bruising to delicate parts of his anatomy.

When the tormented soul regained consciousness, he remembered two things. – He must never again allow consignments to get wet or to be delivered late, and if he valued his life he would have to quickly trace and eliminate the occupants of the blue Jaguar. If they had any evidence at all to identify him, however unlikely this might be, it potentially could lead to JG, his associates in Paisley and the Colombian Cartel.

"Why, oh why, did I ever become involved in this?" thought Ted.

His bowels loosened explosively and his alcohol-befuddled brain began even more slowly than usual, to digest the enormity of his new situation. He crawled on his bloodied hands and scraped knees out of the quarry. Only with extreme difficulty was he able to limp painfully all the miles back to Inverness and the comfort of the Premier Inn.

For obvious reasons he had the good sense to wait until the concierge was away from the reception desk before accessing the building, and making optimum use of the pristine bathroom facilities.

"It is my life or theirs" was his final thought before drifting off into the Land of Nod, the only place now in which he could ever be comfortable.

-Chapter Seventeen-

Laura Brown's job was an interesting one. She acted as Registration Officer for the National Park Authority, spending most of her time in a customer relations capacity at the public counter of the office attached to the Drumkinnon Bay slipway. A bright and vivacious girl in her early twenties, she thoroughly enjoyed her work, meeting as she did some really interesting people who owned the many leisure craft that took to the water throughout the boating season that started on 1 April each year. The computerised records were upgraded recently when charges to use the loch were introduced, but still kept on an ancient old server within the premises. They were backed up to a remote site on a daily basis.

Approximately 5,000 craft were registered with the Park Authority, with about 30% of these broadly classified as speedboats. Plastic cards including a brief description of each vessel were issued for checking purposes each time the Loch Lomond facilities were used, so this information was also held electronically.

The imposition of fairly restrictive speed limits in recent years on some of the English Lakes such as Windermere, had seen many boaters from down south transfer their loyalties to Scotland, where they appreciated the superior facilities on offer at Balloch. That was how Laura had met her English boyfriend, Jonathan, when he first came to register his jet ski.

One Tuesday evening she was settling down with Jon for a cosy evening at home in front of the television. She had just finished her first glass of Sauvignon Blanc – Marlborough, which was her favourite, when the call came.

There had been a break-in at her place of work. As the nominated key holder, her presence was required.

According to the very young and apparently very well-informed police officer who smiled constantly at her and tried shamelessly to chat her up in the squad car, it looked like a pro' job. A glasscutter had been used to gain access and apart for some paper files that had been disturbed there was no other obvious damage. The intruder had even prevented the relatively sophisticated security alarm from going off, and it was only a random check of the premises by a beat constable checking on the Maid of the Loch nightspot nearby that had given the game away.

"Why on earth would anyone break into the slip office?" thought Laura. "It is not as if any cash is held there, and there is little of value on the premises."

As she entered the building, everything looked normal. It was only when she checked under the counter that she realised her old computer was missing. It had been of little intrinsic value, and Laura was already looking forward to a modern replacement, but why would that grubby old box be of interest to anyone?

Ted's associate, Bill from the Millerston area, knew the answer to that one. He had been employed and trained on the technical side by CPU World in Dumbarton Road, but by a strange turn of circumstances his departure had co-incided with the loss of a valuable consignment of the latest super-thin LED televisions.

-Chapter Eighteen-

It took two full weeks for Bill to extract the required file from the stolen box. The data had been encrypted to prevent unauthorised access and all of Bill's expertise together with some assistance from a dodgy pal in Tottenham Court Road, were necessary before he cracked it.

By this time DS Ramsay, who routinely received an incident report for anything that happened on his patch, was beginning to put two and two together. This was no random burglary. It could only mean one thing. James Brown's killing (the fact that it was a murder was now established beyond all doubt) had only been the tip of the iceberg.

Forensic evidence from the Range Rover had been helpful and in most cases would have led to an immediate arrest. In current circumstances, however, more questions than answers were arising and taking everything into consideration it would be some time before the fat lady would have her chance to sing. The intelligence Ramsay had received from his drug squad colleagues made a wider-ranging and protracted investigation more likely than ever.

He reached immediately for his phone and dialled the contact number that he had jotted in his notebook after interviewing the Hunters.

"Mr David Hunter?" "Detective Superintendent Ramsay here… I am afraid I have some bad news for you."

-Chapter Nineteen-

From the wilds of the Highlands to a small basement flat in Edinburgh's Georgian New Town is quite a transition, but Mr and Mrs Hunter and their sons Rory and Stuart were forced to make a first relocation to there within 24 hours.

Safe houses are now rarely provided in the United Kingdom under the Witness Protection Programme. Where they are, it is usually only where there is a very serious risk to an individual who has witnessed a crime being committed. The person will be given a new name and from then on will be referred to only by that new name. Only one police officer will ever know the witness's true name and that will never be revealed in any documents, statements or Court proceedings.

The Hunter family did not quite meet these criteria, but DS Ramsay had to play safe and assume that their identities, and certainly David's because he was named as boat owner in the Loch Lomond records, were now known to the Paisley mob.

Their Colombian masters took no prisoners. If they had even the slightest suspicion that the Hunters could give evidence against any one of those in the supply chain, elimination would be the name of the game. Only last year the Scottish tabloids had made much of the case of a Stevenston resident, when what was left of him had been found legless (in the literal sense, rather than his habitual weekend state) below the Erskine Bridge.

Ramsay briefed David Hunter on a strictly "need to know" basis. He understood the seriousness of his situation and worried about Stuart and Rory, neither of whom he suspected would take kindly to prolonged confinement, isolated from all friends and family.

David himself had taken early retirement from his employment with the local enterprise company some 3 months previously. As far as neighbours were concerned the message was relayed back to them that the family were taking advantage of a last minute Antipodean Cruise bargain, and they would not be returning home for at least 6 months.

Mrs Hunter, under the same pretext, took leave of absence from her place of employment. In reality she thought it unlikely that she would ever be back and was quite relishing the prospect. She had spent far too many years in the workplace and to paraphrase the words of Charles Lamb, feared that "the wood from her desk would enter into her soul." The demands of the workplace were even starting to impinge on her social life and charity work with the Inner Wheel Club, and that was quite unacceptable!

Within a few days, a certain Mr and Mrs Henderson (Frank and Louise) had boarded a flight from Edinburgh heading not for the other side of the world as announced, but instead for a small gite near the home of Dom Perignon in the Champagne district of France, where they intended to lie low until it was safe for them to return.

Their first impressions of rural France at the Louis Nicaise Champagne visitor centre were so favourable and their neighbours so welcoming and generous with the local produce, that the couple would not be in any particular rush to return home anyway.

-Chapter Twenty-

Despite official and parental warnings, Fraser and Callum as Rory and Stuart had become, refused to believe that they were in any danger. After all, they had not seen their attacker who had retrieved his stash and who, presumably, was well out of the country by now.

As part of their cover, the Programme had enrolled them as students at Edinburgh University but they had no intention of completing their courses in History of Art. For as long as the authorities were happy to fund their undergraduate lifestyle they were prepared to play the roles demanded of them. On their occasional visits to lectures they would studiously ignore the oftimes quoted advice given in 1786 by Thomas Jefferson to his son-in-law…

"You are now in a place where the best courses upon earth are within your reach. Such an opportunity you will never again have."

Life in a flat in the Edinburgh New Town wasn't at all bad. With mother and father sojourning amongst the vineyards, they had a double bedroom each and were determined to make the most of the opportunity. Happily men studying History of Art were in a minority, so there was no shortage of impressionable young ladies, eager to make the acquaintance of the young Highlanders.

Before long they had quite a following.

Fraser had taken a particular fancy to Sarah Mackenzie, also a fresher but a year or so older than himself. Sarah was a neighbour who lived nearby in Atholl Crescent, and although she did not broadcast the fact, her father (rather unkindly nicknamed Rudolph) was a rotund High Court Judge as well as a connoisseur of fine wine.

One might have assumed that coming from such a straitlaced background, Sarah would be a shy retiring young lady but this was anything but the case. She had first come to Fraser's attention when one evening after consuming rather too many shots of vodka in the University Union bar, she had climbed, scantily clad, upon the table and performed a quite uninhibited burlesque routine to the obvious enjoyment of all the males present. At the end of her dance, she stretched out her hand to Fraser. She invited him most seductively to climb up onto the table and examine her "Bazookas"!

To his credit Fraser declined to do so, but a close private inspection took place the very next evening when they were both sober and knew exactly what they were doing.

This may not have been quite the opportunity that Thomas Jefferson had in mind, but Fraser marvelled at the wonderful opportunities that his new University life was opening up for him.

Callum was not backward in coming forward either when it came to the ladies, although his approach was subtler. He had spotted a particularly attractive redhead while he was queuing for his student library pass. It didn't take him long to engage her in polite conversation and for her to realise that he had a fine sense of humour. They apparently had a shared interest in sport. In the year of the Olympics they would have had plenty to talk about.

If the truth were told, Callum's interest in the Metabolism of Endurance Athletes was less serious than Fiona's. He had spotted the title of the book she had borrowed from the library, and feigned interest in the subject matter even although his own knowledge was limited to a recent article he had read in the Evening News concerning the demands likely to be put upon track and field athletes at forthcoming events in London. Callum was a convincing sort of fellow.

He was actually beginning to enjoy his course at University, especially when his research work meant an excuse to wander around museums and art galleries at will with the girl of his dreams. He was almost prepared to forget Loch Lomond, to start to forgive the individual who had been responsible for uprooting him and his family from their comfortable life in the Highlands.

And having his parents out of his hair was the icing on the cake. Like his brother, he was free to drink, gamble and generally misbehave to his heart's content.

-Chapter Twenty One-

It was 11 am on 30 December and DS Ramsay was having his 6-monthly case review.

Present with him in a utilitarian conference room of the Strathclyde force's Pitt Street headquarters were the Depute Chief Constable and representatives of SOCA, the Serious Organised Crime Agency.

SOCA's remit is to tackle serious organised crime that affects the UK and its citizens. This includes Class A drugs, people smuggling and human trafficking, major gun crime, fraud, computer crime and money laundering.

The Superintendent was relieved to have them on board, not least because his own Duck Bay investigation was still in progress. He was having difficulty justifying the ever-increasing costs, including those being incurred on ongoing protection of the hapless individuals still considered to be at risk.

SOCA monitored serious career criminals, in some cases for life. The aim was to prevent their criminal activities. The organisation could and would go anywhere in the world in support of that. A street drug trader was often the last in a chain that stretched to the other side of the world and the Agency used all sorts of ways to accumulate first class intelligence, and focus on the main players.

They were expert in hitting criminals where it hurt most. For many successful criminals this worried them more than the prospect of a spell in prison.

Ramsay knew that he would have to be patient. Based on intelligence from SOCA, the finger of suspicion was now being pointed clearly at Edward Fortescue and his known associates. Only in the last week had this been corroborated by other facts coming to light.

The cabin cruiser had been found at last, thanks to fuel leaking to the surface from its watery grave. A close examination again revealed fingerprints of the same known individual and a partial match with one print on the engine cowling of the Hunters' sports boat.

So why, in what after all was a murder investigation and looked like becoming an open and shut case, had Edward Fortescue not even been called in for questioning? - The answer was quite simple; SOCA had bigger fish to fry.

The scale of drug trafficking from South America was now really significant. There had been a total of 584 deaths due to drugs misuse in Scotland alone in 2011, up 99 on the previous year and a 76% increase on 2001.

Our Ted was the spry to catch the mackerel.

He was being tailed but from a distance, and had already provided a mine of useful information.

After a full formal assessment of the risks and consideration of the implications of the Regulation of Investigatory Powers Act, those present in Pitt Street that morning agreed that the status quo should be maintained and Fortescue would remain at large for a further specified period. This was in the reasonable expectation that he would eventually lead them to his controller.

It was assumed that any disclosures by the person under surveillance would be inadvertent and unwitting since even a life sentence for murder would be preferable to the grisly end that invariably came to those of his ilk who grassed.

As Ramsay left the meeting and walked along Sauchiehall Street to catch the Glasgow Underground, he pondered on the day's business. He had been reading in a paper by the National Strategy Information Centre about the correlation between state corruption and organised criminal activity:

This unholy alliance exploits the fragile political, economic and cultural conditions within a country, especially those either in conflict or post-conflict, to create a permanently corrupt state and an outward flow of national wealth to both offshore "tax havens" and major international crime syndicates to fund illicit activities. It is those proceeds of corruption and misappropriated funds that are in many cases used to enable lucrative for-profit activities such as narcotics and money laundering. The majority of efforts to prosecute corrupt individuals and regimes are

conducted government to government. History shows
that this is a long drawn-out process often filled with
stumbling blocks and unforeseen issues.

Ramsay speculated as to whether his professional life
would have been different if governments had deployed
greater resources earlier and at the appropriate level,
and not left poor suckers like him to fall over the
stumbling blocks and deal with the unforeseen
problems.

But still he was a home bird. He had no inclination to
become involved further afield, in rooting out those
seemingly untouchable masterminds who employed
lowly villains and mules like Fortescue. Murder
investigation was his speciality, and not even a trip to
exotic South America would tempt him away from his
Strathclyde patch, where there was more than enough
need for his finely-honed skills to keep him gainfully
employed.

He had been to Machu Pichu once and hadn't been
particularly impressed. He knew it wasn't actually
Colombia, but he didn't really care.

"It was near enough."

Colombia's geographical location near the Equator meant that the climate, although highly variable according to altitude would at times be too hot and humid for him, and the natives were not likely to be friendly.

The rainy season caused by the Intertropical Convergence Zone would also remind him too much of family holidays "doon the watter."

-Chapter Twenty Two-

Sarah Mackenzie was quite pleased with herself. She eventually had found a boyfriend who could present a sober and sensible face to the gentile New Town set that included her father and his august friends, but when it came to behaviour in private he was every bit as wild as herself. She liked that!

She was a risk taker, someone who got a buzz out of breaking the rules. She seized life with both hands, was confident, uninhibited and used to getting her own way.

One morning, shortly after she had moved in with Fraser, she put a proposition to him.

They would hire an open-topped car for a long weekend and venture north so that she could find out a little more about him and where he came from. After all, that would only be fair since Fraser knew everything about her. She had formed the impression that he would talk about anything apart from his past.

"You need to relax a bit," she said, with a sparkle in her eye, "and what better opportunity to do that could there be than an idyllic short break on the Black Isle?"

Why should Fraser refuse? He had been warned several times about the need for discretion, and it was a condition of his present living arrangements that he had signed a legally binding agreement, guaranteeing not to communicate with any of his former neighbours and friends.

His personal opinion, for what it was worth, was that whoever had been chasing them on Loch Lomond that one day in May would have lost interest in them long ago.

"So what harm could there be, in driving past some of his old haunts?"

Although he would not admit it, he was becoming bored with many aspects of life in central Edinburgh. Parking was never easy at the best of times and despite the excellent location of the flat in the city's west end, he missed having a garage.

On-street parking charges in the city centre were on a par with London and the traffic congestion was appalling, mainly due to the enormous and some might say misplaced public investment in a new civic tramway system, completion of which was still some way off. Many motorists were confused by the temporary traffic management arrangements, especially if they were visitors to the city and would drive round and round incessantly, trying to find their way from A to B. Even if they were fortunate enough to have a SatNav system, this was often of little use in the constantly changing dynamics of the situation.

Pedestrians too were inconvenienced by the excavation work all around them as pavements were dug up to allow infrastructure to be installed, and diversions imposed. But not as much as the residents of the medieval cemeteries, whose eternal repose under the roads of the capital didn't turn out to be quite so eternal after all!

The more Fraser thought about it, the more he missed the peace and quiet, fresh air and dark skies at night that only a gentle Highland environment can provide;

also the soft accents of the local people that he knew so well.

When he eventually said yes, Sarah was over the moon with excitement. She knew that her charm offensive was working. After all, she had never met any man who could resist her.

Before Fraser knew it the pair were on the M90, crossing the Forth Bridge with the wind in their hair and the Firth way below them glistening in the early morning sunshine.

A large American cruise ship was anchored off South Queensferry, just below the bridge and to their right. As they watched several of the ship's brightly-coloured tenders were making their way to the shore, carrying some of the 2,000 loud tourists en route to the Capital's Princes Street shops and Castle.

"If it's Saturday it must be Edinboro!"

Sarah and Fraser were glad to be heading in the opposite direction. Their week together in the country was much more appealing. - They hadn't a care in the world.

-Chapter Twenty Three-

With memories of his delightful trip to the remote
Cabrich quarry still uppermost in his mind, Ted was
reluctant ever again to make the long haul to Inverness.
He had settled quite comfortably back into his daily
routine of greasy late breakfast in his local takeaway,
frequent trips to Brokelads, the local bookmaker, and
an Indian carryout in Paisley later in the day. Most
evenings were spent slouched on the sofa watching Sky
Movies, eating cheese and onion crisps and washing it
all down with McEwen's Export.

Aggie McPhee, a hirsute neighbour of indeterminate
gender who preferred the barley bree to the McEwen's,
joined him occasionally in these endeavours. Ted's
relationship with her was more fraternal than romantic,
but that didn't stop the two of them sharing his bed
when the need arose. They were an unlikely couple.
Bedtimes were reminiscent of the hippopotamus advert
running some time ago on Scottish Television.

No-one would have either of them, but what they lacked in personal charisma or fragrance, they made up for in blundering enthusiasm; to that extent they were an ideal if unattractive match for each other.

To straitlaced PC Macleod, who had been brought up on the Isle of Skye and who was unfortunate enough to be on surveillance duties that week, such a lifestyle was beyond his understanding. Nevertheless he recorded each and every sordid detail for later reference.

When the call came, Ted found it most unwelcome.

"Get yer erse up the A9!"

The inestimable Stanley Baxter would have put it more delicately.

"Apparently there was a spot of unfinished business in Inverness that needed Edward's urgent attention."

Scarcely pausing to do more than grab the holdall that was always kept in readiness due to the peripatetic nature of his employment, he managed to move his "erse" with remarkable speed.

When you're not constrained by the niceties of the law or the mores of social responsibility, you can have your pick of vehicle. Even in today's world of steering locks, intruder alarms and tracker devices, a little knowledge and a lot of practice in execution can go a long way - in Ted's case from outside a Victorian villa in Houston in Renfrewshire, all the 185 miles north to Inverness. The fuel economy was remarkable too for a powerful vehicle like a BMW X5 – when someone else was paying.

About three hours later Ted had passed the hamlet of Daviot, switched off the cruise control and started the long descent down into Inverness. In front of him he could see the new Golden Bridge leading to the fine modern Campus of the Highlands and Islands University, the familiar outline of Raigmore Hospital, and the elegant iconic shape of the Kessock Bridge, which crosses over the Moray Firth to the Black Isle.

His SatNav told him to take the first exit at the Caledonian Thistle Football Stadium roundabout and the road that leads west.

Ted wasn't a stranger to the area. Thanks to Laura Brown's excellent record keeping and Bill's skills as a software engineer he was already familiar with the Hunter residence. From his previous clandestine visit he had established that David Hunter was married. He also knew from checks of the publically available electoral roll that there were two sons, although when he called the house was locked up, obviously unoccupied and there was no trace of the inhabitants.

His task this time was to rifle carefully through more cupboards in their home, and try to establish where they had gone. He would also gather together any files or paperwork that would provide a clue to their interests, any clubs or associations where they might be members, and who their friends might be.

He had visited a couple of neighbours after his last trip north, but that had been a singular waste of time. Clearly they didn't know the family's whereabouts and even if they had done so, they were cautious enough not to trust the overweight stranger who looked as if he had lost a recent battle with a demon hairdresser. With his bright red hair he certainly did not fit the expected profile of a long lost relative of the Hunters.

Despite his crumpled business suit, he looked more like a refugee from Rock Ness or the more family-friendly Belladrum Music Festival on a particularly bad day.

.

-Chapter Twenty Four-

Fraser or Rory as he was now known, had by this time confided in Sarah. He knew that he shouldn't, but could not help himself.

He was fed up with constantly having to lie about the past, and fast approaching the point where he himself could not differentiate fact from fiction. Sarah had already tripped him up several times about family details, and enough was enough.

She had taken Rory's news surprisingly well and was relieved that there was a valid reason, however serious, for Fraser's intermittently strange responses to her questions.

So after a few glasses of wine that very first night in their bijou holiday cottage, when they were cuddled up naked in bed with two fine cognacs and watching the sun going down over the water, Rory started to tell her the full story of the Loch Lomond adventure and how it had changed the lives of his family ever since.

Sarah was secretly glad that it had, otherwise with her father's blessing she might still have been dating some balding chinless wonder whose only apparent merit was that he was studying at the Bar.

-Chapter Twenty Five-

JG was becoming impatient with his minion. Ted knew this. He had received another visit.

He was only a couple of days into his latest sojourn in Inverness when he received a letter addressed to a Mr Paddington, inviting him to take a stroll through the "islands" area, down by the River Ness that very evening. The significance of the name Paddington escaped him; to Ted it was simply the latest alias he had been instructed to use.

About 8pm Fortescue left his waterside hotel, crossed the suspension bridge further downstream and made his way away from Inverness Castle towards the islands, much promoted by the local tourist board as a "quiet walking area where visitors can unwind and be at one with nature".

Even the hardened Ted could not help being impressed by the young grey heron he saw stalking the bank in the evening sunshine, and the two elderly fisherman he saw fly-fishing expertly from near the hut on the opposite shore.

The river waters in this area are crystal clear and you can see every stone on the river bed; quite a contrast thought Ted to his local stretch of the Cart, where despite the Scottish Environmental Protection Agency's best endeavours, one was still more likely to catch a shopping trolley or a serious infection, than a wild salmon.

As Ted crossed the final bridge to the furthermost island in the chain, he must subconsciously have absorbed some of the atmosphere of the place. He started having uncharacteristic thoughts, such as wondering if promoting tourism to encourage incomers to visit this unspoilt area would destroy the very attractiveness of the place.

But perhaps he was worrying unnecessarily? - He had passed only one dog walker and one jogger so far that evening, and remarkably for Ted he noted that the area was litter-free.

On the Ness island furthest upstream, there is a small seating area where visitors can savour the power of the mighty Highland river as it divides and water surges noisily past on two sides. The area is popular with young couples for wedding photographs seeking, weather permitting, to include an authentic Highland setting in the record of their happy day.

There is also a large tree trunk nearby that local wags have carved with some skill, into the shape of the Loch Ness Monster. Ted by this time was feeling the effects of the pack of strong lagers he had imbibed en route, so after relieving himself somewhat freely on the shore he stretched out impressively on the broad back of the Monster and closed his eyes for a brief snooze.

PC Macleod watched this incongruous scene from a riverside hide that he had chanced upon, further up the river and some 100 yards away.

He saw two cyclists dismount behind some rhododendrons, and creep up on Ted. After gagging him brutally, they tied him firmly to the log where he lay. The pair then proceeded with some difficulty to drag "the Monster" to a pivot point at the edge of the river where they levered its head, and Ted's by default, into the fast flowing water. They repeated this dunking process several times until Ted lay motionless, before whipping him back into life with willow branches that they found on the shore. They eventually released him to stumble back towards the lights of Inverness.

The Highland torture left few physical marks except bruises where he had been tied, but its emphatic message was again clear.

"He needed to move faster in resolving the loose ends affecting the northern supply chain."

PC Macleod could have intervened at any moment to save Ted from what he thought was going to be an unpleasant end, but he was under orders and powerless to intervene. Doing nothing ran contrary to everything he had been taught during his Sunday School days on Skye, and he felt bad.

When he had volunteered for surveillance duties, he had no perception of what it would involve.

What would tomorrow bring?

-Chapter Twenty Six-

"Mr Paddington" woke up late the next morning. Not surprisingly, he had a monster headache both physiologically and metaphorically. His good Loake shoes, purchased only recently in Inverness, were still squelching from their riparian adventure at the Ness the previous evening. Like their wearer, they were a bit off colour.

Using material obtained on Ted's second visit to the Hunters' home, JG's more trusted staff had provided him with a fairly detailed spreadsheet analysis of the family's known activities, club memberships, and leisure pursuits. He was also in possession of some photographs in an album taken from a bookcase that clearly had been missed earlier by those sanitising the property.

Even with this wealth of information, Ted was none the wiser. All he could do was trek around known contacts in the Moray Firth area, hoping to learn something about his quarry's whereabouts, but without arousing suspicion. He knew it wouldn't be easy, but he had to keep going.

The local sports and leisure club had been his first port of call. The petite young receptionist on the desk that day felt intimidated by the large and unattractive man staring down at her with his tiny eyes and enormous double chin. She listened politely to his question about the Hunters, and after referring briefly to her computer, informed him that there were no current members with that surname. She apologised but said that the Data Protection Act applied and it was not the policy of the Fit and Well Organisation to disclose personal details anyway, even of former members.

Ted looked up and noticed the CCTV camera above the desk. He thought better of remonstrating with the young lady, winked menacingly at her as might a Hollywood casting director, and left.

-Chapter Twenty Seven-

Meanwhile, back in Glasgow DS Ramsay was again carrying out a case review.

PC Macleod at his own request had been recalled from surveillance duties, apparently suffering from stress, but in reality having been sickened by the nature of the surveillance.

His replacement, a Detective Inspector Turner was altogether a more hardened career cop, having been brought up in Port Glasgow and having spent most of his career to date in the same Division.

He was recognised as a bit of a rough diamond, someone who was more than a match for most of the criminals on his patch. He had worked with DSR before and together they were a formidable force.

Ramsay could still have brought in Fortescue at any time. Ted's ineptitude for the criminal role was staggering and he left a trail of evidence wherever he went. It was only the prospect of him exposing further connections that allowed his freedom to continue. At least the police officer knew where he was at all times, and at the moment he seemed to be more of a danger to himself than to others. His exploits could fill a book.

Ramsay received regular reports too about the Hunters, and their lives in the Programme. He knew that they were managing to maintain a low profile and that to date, as far as he was aware, there had been no compromising of their anonymity.

He had been informed of course about the boys' student antics, but wasn't too concerned. It added a touch of realism. He almost admitted to being slightly envious himself of their lifestyle. As long as they weren't too outrageous and kept out of the public eye, he wouldn't be the one to spoil their fun!

-Chapter Twenty Eight-

In August each year, usually on the third Saturday and when tidal conditions are favourable, a Raft Race is held on the River Ness.

This raises thousands of pounds for charities as local organisations in fancy dress race interesting homemade creations in a series of heats from one end of the city to another. The streets around the centre of the city can be thronged with locals and tourists alike, cheering on their favourites and in a good year there is seldom a space to be had on any of the several bridges that cross the river.

The foreign tourists, in particular, like to stand on the bridges and many have their photographs taken as they pose imperiously next to brightly coloured floral hanging baskets, in front of Inverness Castle. For our North American cousins this is what "doing Scotland" is all about.

"How many thousands, tens or hundreds of thousands of such photographs circulate around the globe?"

In this festive atmosphere, with the mood fuelled by the various attractive watering holes whose premises overlook the scene, it is traditional for whole families to congregate and enjoy several hours socialising at, or even in, the river.

This year, the weather was unusually favourable and the City looked at its best. The crowds were swollen by overseas visitors spending a day in the Highlands as part of their cruise to Europe and the Mediterranean; Inverness happily being within easy reach of the deep-water port of Invergordon.

Rory had paddled for his former school at the previous year's event and could not resist the opportunity to join the crowds on such a glorious day. Naturally Sarah had to accompany him.

They watched three of the raft races from the pedestrian suspension bridge at about the midpoint of the course. The bridge swayed with all the sightseers, and the volunteer race marshals tried in vain to stop more spectators joining them, in case it became unsafe.

The swaying of the bridge wouldn't have improved the quality of the photographs that were being taken. Rory and Sarah, however, didn't take any photographs. As usual they had eyes only for each other.

They stood for quite a while, chatting away happily and quite oblivious to all around them. Had they been more perceptive, they may have noticed that they were being scrutinised by a stout red-haired gentleman watching the races from the comfort of a picnic chair on the riverbank near the end of their bridge. He had a can of Tennents in his hand and was dressed rather too formally for the occasion, although he wore trainers on his feet, which looked more than a bit peculiar.

"I am hungry," said Sarah. - She was also a little bored with the time delay between races, but didn't say so.

"You stay here and watch the next race, and I'll pop along to the supermarket and get us something to eat."

She skipped merrily along to the end of the bridge, and started to walk towards the town.

She passed Ted's chair en route, but he was nowhere to be seen. Several empty beer cans were discarded on the grass.

-Chapter Twenty Nine-

The last race came.........and went.

The race organisers aided by volunteers from one of the City's four Rotary Clubs were already using a mobile crane to remove competitors' rafts from the water, and the crowds had started to disperse.

Rory waited until the last spectator had gone, but there was still no sign of Sarah.

He was normally cool in a crisis, but this was different. He followed what he thought would be her route to the nearest supermarket, and then retraced his steps. He even made a diversion running along the busy pavement to the waterfront bar outside which the prizegiving for rafters was taking place. She wasn't there either.

"How could she have vanished into thin air?" He knew she was often impulsive and unpredictable, but this was quite out of character.

There was no reply to her mobile phone, and he knew that she had charged it that morning. "Perhaps she had lost her phone, but if so, why hadn't she returned? She wouldn't have gone anywhere without letting him know. She did not know anyone in the city. Something serious must be amiss."

And this entire mess was his fault. If anything happened to her, he could never forgive himself. Only a fool would have breached the quite explicit terms of his Witness Protection Order. His mind was racing and he trembled with fear as he realised that there already had been one murder.

"Please God, don't let there be another!

-Chapter Thirty-

Detective Inspector Turner was no slouch, but had to be quick off his mark.

He had noticed Ted taking a particular interest in a couple on the bridge, and had thought nothing of it at first. Then the penny dropped. He recognised Rory from his photograph in the Duck Bay file.

When Sarah left, the detective temporarily switched surveillance to Rory, on the basis that he was the person most at risk. Turner was standing on the first section of the bridge watching him when he noticed with a sinking feeling that Ted, his official target, had disappeared in the direction of the city centre.

The DI was following discreetly behind him when Ted suddenly broke into a run.

The policeman followed, although at some distance.

Ted's reasoning was quite simple.

"Kidnap the girl and use her as bait to ensnare all three of the boaters."

It was a stroke of genius, even although he said it himself.

His car was parked where he had left it the previous evening, in the private carpark adjoining the Palace Hotel, which also overlooks the river.

Sarah was rendered unconscious as she approached the carpark entrance. So expertly that she didn't have time to scream. Ted made short work of bundling her limp body unceremoniously into the vehicle, although her long suntanned legs didn't make this at all easy.

A breathless DI Turner arrived on the scene only in time to see their departure via the opposite end of the hotel carpark.

One of Sarah's favourite designer shoes lay forlorn on the tarmac.

-Chapter Thirty One-

It would be wrong to say that DS Ramsay was angry when he heard from DI Turner. His temper was fiercesome.

He now had no alternative but to alert the local force, which would probably put out an "all units" call to find the kidnapper and his victim. They would wade in with their size tens, and potentially ruin several years of meticulous case planning and collaboration with SOCA. Not only would the cat be out of the bag, it would be meowing half way to South America!

By this time, Rory had made his way breathlessly to the nearest police station and reported Sarah missing. The desk sergeant, when informed of the circumstances followed procedure to the letter.

He immediately made a secure call to the Witness Protection Programme. Rory was removed to a safe house for his own protection, despite his protestations that he was responsible for Sarah's predicament. It didn't matter what he said and how much he pleaded, there was no way that he would be allowed to assist in the search activity that was immediately organised.

The hours passed and soon the sun was setting in a warm red glow over the glorious hills around Glen Affric.

Such is the beauty of the Glen, the location chosen by Sir Edwin Landseer in 1851 for his iconic portrait of the Monarch of the Glen, and now designated a National Nature Reserve, that there are few individuals who are not moved by the magnificence of its rugged hills and lochs; also the acres of old Scots pine that give even the casual visitor a glimpse of what the ancient Caledonian Pine Forest that once covered most of the Highlands would have looked like.

The Glen is about 30 miles long and (going west from Inverness), stretches from near Cannich in Strathglass to Kintail on the west coast.

Despite its world-class scenery and obvious tourism potential, it is relatively sparsely populated, and has been so since the 1780s saw whole families forced to abandon their traditional subsistence farming on poor soil, and make way for sheep farming which offered a more remunerative use of their land.

It hadn't taken long for Ted to leave Inverness and head for the remoteness of one of Scotland's most scenic areas.

He (or rather JG on his behalf) had planned for such an eventuality and the small two-man tent sharing the boot of the car with the still comatose Sarah, would come in very handy.

They were approaching the turn-off for Tomich and less than 4 miles from the start of the Glen, when Sarah came round. She awoke with a start, quite sick with fear when she realised her predicament. Being trussed up like a turkey, she couldn't move a muscle, and her neck was throbbing with blinding pain.

She quickly realised that she must have been abducted. The vehicle she was travelling in was being driven fast along country roads. Her mind raced as she thought of the consequences. As an avid reader of crime novels, she knew that the prognosis was not good. There was seldom a happy ending for the heroine of such a story.

Sarah was aware that someone had covered her with a blanket, so being deprived of sight as well as mobility tended to narrow her options. She listened hard, but heard very little in the darkness.

"Where was her Rory?" "Only he would know that she was missing.

-Chapter Thirty Two-

Some might say that it was good policing by the Highland Constabulary that resulted in the kidnap vehicle being spotted on the Glen Affric Road that evening. In reality, it was more a case of good fortune.

DI Turner had passed on the vehicle details that were already known to the police to the local Division, and within minutes a plain clothes patrol based in Dingwall had spotted the black Audi speeding past the Bogroy Inn at Inchmore, heading west.

They had tailed the car for about ten miles, and were in touch intermittently by phone with DS Ramsay, who relayed instructions to them. They then pulled back, handing over surveillance to a local plainclothes officer who would remain at some distance but establish their precise destination. Secrecy was of the essence.

DI Turner himself followed on up the Cannich Road in a support vehicle with a cohort of uniformed personnel.

He took time en route to properly plan the details and consult with those further up the line of command, not least because this would be a high visibility operation with several agencies involved.

Although the girl would not be enjoying her night out with Big Edward, her life was not considered to be at risk. She was far too valuable to the Cartel.

It is a pity that Sarah did not know this.

-Chapter Thirty Three-

The vehicle had stopped.

Her heart was pounding within her, as if to burst.

When the cover was pulled back all her worst fears
were confirmed.

Standing before her was a beast of a man. - In his hand,
a gun.

They were parked in a secluded clearing some distance
off the road. There was a full moon so she saw quite
clearly. Her eyes had been accustomed to the darkness
of the boot.

He raised his gun and pointed directly at her head. Her
involuntary response was to vomit in abject terror.

"Out", he said, manhandling her so roughly that her
blouse became quite undone, and depositing her, still
bound up, on the heather.

"You and I have unfinished business."

He then proceeded to put up the tent.

Sarah lay where she was, sobbing uncontrollably.

-Chapter Thirty Four-

There is not much room in a basic two-man tent. Sarah
was no longer fully bound, but she was shackled to the
loathsome fellow, which was worse. He had allowed
her one toilet break in the bushes, but had kept his gun
and therefore his eyes trained on her throughout. She
did not know his plans for her, and that made things
insufferable. She was constantly imagining the worst.

What a vile creature he was, snoring away happily at
her side after downing one too many shots of the
Macallan whisky taken from the glove compartment of
the car. She could smell his breath and it wasn't
pleasant.

The young woman felt dirty, desperate and degraded.

Unsurprisingly, she did not feel inclined to sleep.

Mercifully cloud cover now obscured the full moon. At
least she didn't have to look at his ugly face.

It was pitch dark outside, and eerily quiet apart from the noise of the occasional nocturnal animal.

-Chapter Thirty Five-

Sarah must have nodded off briefly despite her steely resolve. She certainly had no intention of actually sleeping, but could not help herself.

Then in an instant she was wide-awake, experiencing an intense bright light shining down on her from above. At the same time the tent appeared to move. The ground vibrated below her. A fearsome wind blew.

- It was an epic of Biblical proportions.

"He has shot me", she thought. "This must be what happens at The End."

Then she realised that cuddly Ted was still snoring at her side.

"There was no way that he would be allowed into Heaven."

"Was she perhaps in Hell?"

-Chapter Thirty Six-

DS Ramsay was becoming accustomed to the high life. Two hundred feet above the forest floor, he looked down from the chopper on the Old Scots Pines and the tiny green tent pitched in the lonely clearing about 100 yards from a recently built forestry road.

DI Turner and four armed officers were fully deployed in the trees around the clearing, so there would be no escape this time for Ted.

Ramsay's only worry was the unpredictability of his target, not known for the maturity of his responses, and how he would react to being cornered. Would he let the girl go? Would he harm her?

The Detective Superintendent reached for the megaphone.

"This is the police." "Come out slowly with your hands held high."

A few moments later the flap of the tent opens. Ted emerges looking extremely dishevelled. He struggles to untie himself from Sarah.

Ramsay is alarmed to see, however, that he is armed. He is holding a weapon, a handgun, to the young woman's head. She looks white with fear. Her clothes are crumpled and in disarray as if she has slept in them, which of course she has.

His squad have been briefed for such an eventuality. They know that the priority is to rescue Sarah in one piece and to capture Fortescue alive if at all possible. SOCA has further plans for him, but this will not be easy.

Sarah, however, is a tall and strong young woman, and with a keen intelligence.

Just as things are looking dangerous, and at some considerable risk to herself, she contrives to stumble shoeless in the heather and unbalances Ted. He momentarily drops his aim.

In a textbook response his gun is shot instantly from his hand by one of the marksmen.

DS Ramsay sighs with relief. It is a better outcome than he ever could have hoped for.

A bonus is that there is no mobile phone signal in that remote part of the glen, so the authorities' operational planning for dealing with the Cartel should still be viable.

-Chapter Thirty Seven-

The next morning a custody officer from Highland Constabulary opening his cell door startled Fortescue from his slumber.

The Accident and Emergency Department of Raigmore Hospital in Inverness had patched up his hand, and the dose of local anaesthetic he had been given meant that the slight gunshot wound was not troubling him too much. He was more concerned about the Court appearance that past experience told him would inevitably follow his apprehension.

Having washed and dressed with a degree of difficulty, he was therefore surprised to be taken, not to the Courthouse but to a meeting room where a number of officers were seated around a large oval table.

He was not introduced to the assembled company, but had to listen while a proposition was put to him. A duty solicitor had been provided, and helped to explain some of the details that were unclear to Ted.

In essence, if he assisted the officers dealing with the drug enforcement, he "might" have this factor taken into account when his own case came to Court. There would be no guarantees. There could be none. After all, the charges would include murder and there was compelling evidence of his guilt.

He was presented with this and knew that the game was a bogey. Failure to go along with this plea bargain would almost certainly mean that he would be in jail for the rest of his natural life.

Ted was sweating again. He thought long and hard about the consequences. It was "make your mind up" time, but that was never his forte. Had he been back out in the community, he would not for even a second have considered the offer. His life expectancy would be very short.

Despite the relative coolness of the room, his perspiration was forming large damp patches now on his shirt, and he had to mop his brow constantly. What should he do?

His mouth was dry and his head was sore. There was no one telling him what to do except the gloomy looking lawyer sitting alongside him and already looking forward to his lunchtime refreshment.

The reality of Ted's situation took even longer than usual to sink in. It was as if the scene was developing in slow motion before his eyes.

"You may never be released from prison. You should be safe behind bars, outwith the clutches of the Cartel. What have you to lose?"

In his naivety, Fortescue listened to this figure of authority. He followed what he said hook, line and sinker. After all in Ted's case there was some truth in the saying: "the accused that represents himself has a fool for a client!"

Later that day he started to sing like a canary.

-Chapter Thirty Eight-

As every good detective knows, it is the small things that can make a difference.

Like the student card that fell out of Sarah's pocket as Ted was struggling to manoeuvre the unconscious student's long legs into his vehicle on Ness Walk after the raft race.

Ted picked it up, but did not immediately realise the significance of this.

Nevertheless he had reported it in to JG on his mobile phone just before the signal was lost at the start of Glen Affric.

Ted knew his victim only by appearance and her association with Rory, but JG, still unaware that Fortescue had failed in his mission, now knew her identity. That knowledge was power, and the leverage it gave him would prove invaluable.

"Her father would be the first to know."

-Chapter Thirty Nine-

The Honourable Forbes Mackenzie had just returned from a dinner hosted by one of the smaller, some might claim exclusive, law practices in Edinburgh. It had been a splendid evening in an upmarket restaurant just off Rose Street, an establishment renowned not only for the authenticity of its French cuisine but also for the variety and quality of the fine wines on offer from mine host's ample cellar.

Mine host's waistline was ample too, but that came with the territory. He persisted in regaling the assembled company with his many tales of "derring-do." On his most recent hunting trip across the Channel he had bagged a wild boar. He had preserved the unfortunate animal's head for posterity, and brought it home with him to be mounted above the cocktail bar. Before long the majority of his customers that evening were wishing that a similar fate had befallen another bore.

Forbes meanwhile had merrily quaffed the Brouilly, the Santenay and the Puligny-Montrachet, and of course all of this was done in the interests of academic research. Just exactly for what he couldn't quite remember, but he and his new chum, Jeremy from the firm hosting the evening, had been the last to leave. It is fair to say that like Tam O' Shanter and the landlord's wife, they grew fonder of each other as the evening progressed and as the vino collapso flowed.

Just as well that they left when they did, because it was almost 3am when Jeremy's driver dropped the by now barely-coherent Forbes off outside his town house. After the self-indulgent night he had enjoyed, he could hardly remember his own vintage, let alone those shown on the labels of the obscenely priced bottles.

He remembered a song from his childhood and started singing in a loud voice, much to the annoyance of his chauffeur:

"Why did the crocodile weep, boo hoo?

Sitting on a stile

Just beside the Nile.

Had he a pain in his poor little tum?

Nobody wanted to be a new chum!

The driver (perhaps understandably) didn't want to be "a chum" for one moment longer than he needed to. He assisted by turning Forbes' key in the front door lock, forcefully declined his invitation to join him in a dram, and beat a hasty retreat once he had ensured as instructed that his passenger was safely inside the property.

Forbes crossed the grand entrance hall, and made his way to the library. It was his intention there to partake of some vintage port, before retiring replete to his bedchamber. His bloodshot eyes peered across the room in search of his favourite decanter. – It wasn't in its normal place. "Where could it be?"

Just then, he noticed that his comfortable swivel armchair was also facing away from him. No one else but the Judge ever dared to sit in it. Something was not right. He reached out in the semi-darkness to turn it around….

And froze on the spot!

His hand had touched a piece of cold steel. Even in the relative darkness he could see what looked like a semi-automatic weapon. It was attached to the comprehensively tattooed arm of a muscle-bound gentleman of Eastern European extraction.

He was ensconced comfortably in Forbes' personal armchair, with his hobnail boots having already scored the polished surface of his expensive mahogany desk.

"Bonsoir Your Honour," he said in a thick accent. "I am not Russian, but they do so love to play a particular brand of roulette in that country. – Will you play?"

-Chapter Forty-

After her rescue from the Glen, the police had no reason to detain Sarah in Inverness for longer than 12 hours. She told DI Turner all that she knew, which wasn't very much. She was warned quite forcefully that despite her ordeal she must maintain strict confidentiality and trust no one. She would be re-united in due course with Rory who, somewhat chastened, now realised the extent of his irresponsibility in involving Sarah in his private life.

Rory's relief at seeing Sarah physically unharmed was profound, although he noticed privately that she now had developed a worrying tendency to look about her whenever she heard anyone approaching. He appreciated this because his own father had a similar tendency, one acquired some years ago as a result of a painful assault and mugging from behind by an unseen and cowardly thug in the lawless city of Barcelona.

Such tourist crimes were accepted as part of everyday life in that city, but Rory believed that there was very much more that the authorities could do to clean up their patch. His father would never again help to bolster their visitor numbers; indeed he had spent much of the time since his hospitalisation doing what he could to deter his friends from ever visiting the capital city of the autonomous community of Catalonia.

Rory resolved to make amends and minimise any psychological damage to his girlfriend. Instead of returning that night to Edinburgh the pair of them spent a wonderful evening in a boutique hotel in Inverness; a hotel gaining all sorts of awards for the artistry of its celebrity French chef, not to mention its 5-star accommodation and giant hot tub on each balcony.

It was not until the following day that they travelled south, this time in a less conspicuous Vauxhall Astra. The three-hour journey was uneventful, with only one stop at Bruar for a double espresso for the driver, so that he could maintain his caffeine level.

They had tried to ring the old Judge en route, but his landline seemed to be out of order, so they would pay him a quick visit. On a matter of principle, he had never joined the digital revolution, and refused to purchase a mobile.

The word tablet for him meant only one thing - the fudge-like sweet that his old grandmother used to make on high days and holidays, with sugar and Campbell's condensed milk. Or was it evaporated milk? He could no longer remember.

"What need would an old fogey like him have for new technology anyway?"

They arrived in Atholl Crescent about 4pm.

-Chapter Forty One-

Sarah had a horrible feeling as she opened the front door.

Nothing was out of place, but the house was strangely quiet. It would be unusual for her father to be out at that time of day.

"Where could he be?"

She checked the library, usually his favourite haunt. He wasn't there. She noticed that his armchair was not in its usual location, but didn't think anything of it. His daily desk diary that he kept meticulously gave no clue to his whereabouts.

She checked the dishwasher in the kitchen, and it was chock full of the usual dirty crockery.

"He had clearly been in earlier in the day, so perhaps he had simply popped out for a stroll? After all, like most lawyers he was a law unto himself."

Rory by this time had settled down on the well-upholstered sofa in the lounge. Before long Sarah had joined him and the pair of them were locked in a passionate embrace.

They must have nodded off, because it was around midnight before Sarah awoke with a start. There was still no sign of the old man.

"Where could he be at this time of night?"

They wandered through to the kitchen, and raided the well-stocked fridge for a midnight feast. Only then did Rory notice that the small light on the telephone handset on the wall was flashing, indicating that a message had been received.

The message was somewhat garbled, but its import was clear. Rory felt the hairs rise on the back of his neck.

There would be no sleep for either of them again that night.

-Chapter Forty Two-

DS Ramsay was in a bit of a quandary. His sleep had
been interrupted by a priority call from Edinburgh
initiated by Rory calling the emergency helpline, and
he wasn't sure what to make of it.

As things would have it, Turner had already reported in
and provided information about the abduction of the
Judge. From his vehicle parked in the Edinburgh
Crescent he had been awaiting the arrival of Rory and
Sarah from Inverness. Despite the City Council having
reduced the street lighting locally to save energy, he
could not fail to notice the old fellow being bundled
unceremoniously into the back of a Transit van that was
parked at the kerb outside his terraced home.

Fortunately, rather than intervening to rescue the
elderly man, DI Turner had used his initiative and
tailed the van across town, to an anonymous tenemental
property near to Leith Docks and within smelling range
of the local tandoori restaurant. There he remained on

surveillance while another officer was posted to watch the comings and goings at Atholl Crescent.

Poor Forbes was having a miserable time, to put it mildly.

First he was convinced that he was going to die playing a stupid game of Russian roulette, and then he found himself in a cold damp cellar being tortured by two thugs who clearly thought he had knowledge of a family from up North called the Hunters. He didn't. He genuinely had never heard of them, but his two inquisitors wouldn't take no for an answer. They continued relentlessly to ask him the same inane questions.

"Where were the Hunters, and when would they return?"

Even although he was still partially anaesthetised from consuming so much alcohol, he found the pain of the beatings excruciating.

From time to time his tormentors left the room apparently to seek and receive orders by telephone from someone else, but still they returned and the questions and the torture continued. Over and over again. Without mercy.

During the brief periods of respite, Forbes Mackenzie lay on the hard grey slabs of the cellar floor, shivering with fear and cold and seeing no escape from a dire situation. Even in the gloom of the cellar he could see that his extremities were already blue.

From DI Turner's point of view, these calls seeking instruction from on high were extremely valuable. They had lasted long enough for one of the calls eventually to be traced, and this constituted yet another line of compelling evidence that would be passed in due course to the procurator fiscal and other jurisdictions.

Had Forbes Mackenzie known that, he might have struggled to remain alive for just a little longer. Unfortunately his body eventually decided for him that enough was enough.

By dawn he had choked on his own vomit and shuffled off this mortal coil.

-Chapter Forty Three-

Jose Maria Serrano, who coincidentally shared the same name as the first President of the Republic of Colombia, he who sanctioned the first Colombian Constitution of 1886, was himself used to being in a position of authority.

His early years had been spent in the slums of Bucaramanga, the country's sixth biggest metropolitan city, where as legend has it dog ate dog and the poorest in society had to settle for what was left. He had been orphaned at the age of 14, and lived on his wits on the streets until desperate to improve his status in life he fell in with a bad crowd and eventually moved with them to the sprawling, high altitude capital city, Bogota.

There in the fourth most populous Latin American city of more than 7.8m souls, the tall and imposing character put any moral scruples he had aside and forged a remarkable career for himself in the drugs business. As the four main trafficking Cartels grew and established for themselves what was effectively becoming a new social class in that country, he had skilfully positioned himself to climb rapidly up the ladder and to extract maximum personal gain at every step.

The Republic of Colombia's motto was "Libertad y Orden," but Serrano still had the balls to make his own arrangements.

With cocaine sourced from the jungle at as little as $1,500 per kilo and tradeable on the streets of the USA for $50,000, it was little wonder that this streetwise operator soon came to the attention of the drug barons, and they collaborated to mutual advantage. The skill, as Jose Maria knew only too well, was to assess the risks, find someone else naïve or desperate enough to shoulder those risks, and sit back and enjoy the rewards. There was also the small matter of using arm's length individuals to police and enforce his operations.

He himself didn't normally ask too many questions. He simply paid for services rendered and oversaw the Cartel's logistics and money laundering operations. He had become quite expert over the years in financial matters and with major sums deposited in at least four tax havens he slept soundly at night, knowing that diversification had spread the risk around and that he had chosen his investment vehicles with discretion.

Only once had he learned that an offshore fund manager had breached the strict code of confidentiality that was essential if the Cartel's deposits were to remain secure, and Jose Maria had ensured that the individual paid with his life "para animar a los otros."

There was also the small matter of tax evasion. Despite the threat of forced tax haven disclosures being sought by some European countries, the Cartel under Serrano had never paid a peso.

He knew only too well that the Colombian National Police had been effective in their crackdown on trafficking within his country. The drugs trade had lost a lot of good operatives, but paradoxically this had worked to Jose Maria's personal advantage. Over 100 drug lords in each of the last 10 years had been captured and extradited, leaving more business opportunities for well-organised and resilient survivors like Serrano.

There was an almost unbelievable retaliatory campaign of violence across Colombia involving wholesale murders, assassinations, and even the killing of Presidential candidates; which would be unthinkable in any Western European democracy.

Despite all of this and the authorities' many counter measures, a thriving trade in illegal substances persisted, and in a perverse way was a mainstay of life for poor Colombian farmers. It was no longer easy, however, to ship out commercial quantities of any drug, because most countries were becoming wise to what were previously tricks of the trade known only to a few. Serrano's Cartel tended to do their own thing, eschewing concealment of illegal substances below the waterline of ships in favour of more imaginative methods.

Underwater caches meant significant risks to divers as they worked to hide or retrieve consignments. Without announcing the fact, more and more mainstream harbours across the globe had installed advanced electronics to monitor movements both above and below water. Some even used a type of sonar to detect illicit diving work. As well as the risk of discovery, a few of these systems generated underwater noise, painful to anyone in the vicinity and in extreme cases capable of causing permanent hearing loss. One of Serrano's nephews had found this out to his cost.

Nevertheless, new markets were opening up abroad all the time, and the rewards from supplying the traditional markets such as mainland Europe and the United Kingdom remained considerable. Customer demand in general seemed insatiable and the Cartel's activities were as well managed as any business. They even had their own privately funded market research to optimise sales.

Where local demand at street level was perceived to be less than optimal, they employed their own Shockwave methodology, defined in physics as propagating "disturbances with enough energy to neutralise any opposition."

Their tactics would make any Mafioso proud.

-Chapter Forty Four-

Serrano had served his time in most parts of the organised crime world. He knew his onions. His nostrils invariably would be the first to detect a bad smell from afar.

He chose occasionally to visit his more senior field operatives in foreign countries, especially if he had had a whiff of something that wasn't quite right. Whenever he flew, it was naturally on the most expensive ticket, and complete with sycophantic entourage.

Luz Marina Serrano accompanied her husband on British Airways flight BA 147 from Aeropuerto Eldorado in Bogota. Fifteen years his junior, she exuded elegance and charm. Of Latin appearance with characteristic chestnut-brown hair, long eyelashes and dark soulful eyes, Serrano had spotted her in the chorus line of the Teatro Cristobal Colon. She had a lovely smile.

She, like Jose Maria came from the wrong side of the tracks. Her family were poor as church mice, so it was no surprise that she was impressed by the tall aristocratic-looking gentleman that one day appeared at the Stage door of the splendid old neoclassical theatre.

She really had no idea who he was because like so many in the underworld he presented two completely different personae; so charming and affable when he was off duty, but aloof and totally self-centred in the cold light of day.

By the time that Luz Marina saw the light and realised just what a cruel and heartless operator she was involved with, it was too late. A whirlwind wedding and a fairy tale honeymoon on a private yacht in the Bahamas were behind her. She was dripping with jewellery, but like the first (sadly and quite suddenly deceased) Mrs Serrano, the time had already come when she would gladly have given up her trophy wife status and swapped all the expensive bling in the world for a drawerful of costume jewels and a return to her former happy existence on the stage. She knew however that such thoughts were tantamount to high treason.

Even in the pampered confines of the first class lounge of the aircraft, she was reminded of her husband's dark side. A young and personable air steward had made the mistake of chatting to this most attractive young woman with a figure to die for, whose presence in his plane was brightening up his day. He had watched her delicate silk blouse rise and fall as she drifted in and out of sleep in the dimly lit cabin. He had moved a little closer to her, as close as he dared; so close that he could not fail to notice her exquisite eau de parfum and the warmth of her finely toned body.

He watched discreetly as she snoozed. At one point when she stirred he was seen by Jose Maria to whisper something quietly in her diamond-studded ear.

That was the final straw.

All that in fact the steward had done was to quietly ask his passenger "Would Madam care for another glass of bubbly?" but the ensuing row enveloped the cabin and awakened all the other passengers.

This, of course, was the last thing that the steward wished to happen, but he did not know with whom he was dealing, or allow for the hot-blooded Serrano's fiery Latin temperament.

It was already 2am. Soon the plane would be landing in London, and Luz Marina hoped that her attentive and handsome steward would keep well away from her jealous husband.

She had secretly enjoyed the young man's company, flirting outrageously with him whenever her husband's back was turned. She fluttered the long eyelashes that had encouraged many a suitor from the boards of the Teatro, and even allowed her flimsy blouse to slip dangerously from one shoulder; but no matter how much she wanted to, which was a lot, she dared not give this fit young man any further encouragement – for both their sakes.

-Chapter Forty Five-

Even after such an early morning arrival in the UK, the Serranos as befitting their station in life were met by an attaché from the Colombian Embassy in Knightsbridge and chauffeured directly to a private residence that their taxpayers maintained near Sloane Square for visiting dignitaries.

To the world at large the Colombian contingent was just another trade mission (as indeed it was), but Her Majesty's Security Services already had their suspicions about the arrogant South American. On a previous visit his time in Great Britain had coincided with an upsurge in incidents of violent crime. Nothing could be proven at the time, but a subsequent anonymous tip-off (eventually found to have come from a rival gangmaster in Bogota), meant that Serrano's every move would be watched this time from the moment the delegation entered the country.

With the co-operation of Airport Security, a miniature surveillance device had therefore been covertly inserted into a piece of hand luggage belonging to Jose Maria.

-Chapter Forty Six-

After a late breakfast the following day, Luz Marina spent the obligatory hour or so getting her war paint on. This she did from habit rather than from any need to do so, since her healthy diet and pampered lifestyle meant that a simple shower in the morning was more than adequate to set her skin aglow. Indeed such was her earlier appearance in the shower that Jose Maria chose to join her, and to help her with the body lotion afterwards.

He would often chuckle as he thought of the old maxim "Ahorrar agua, ducha con una amiga."

Luz Marina's husband looked up from the pages of Forbes Magazine and watched proprietorially as she slowly dressed. He knew that he could refuse her nothing. Not even her request to be dropped off at Harrods and given free rein to shop until she dropped.

This meant that when Serrano left a couple of hours later for his trip to Edinburgh, he was accompanied only by his driver and a stocky gentleman with a military background, who like Serrano had originated from an impoverished area of Bucaramanga. Since his army days Paulo had seen much active service, but none of it was legitimate. Unarmed combat was his speciality, but no less lethal than when he carried a weapon.

Serrano had owed his life to Paulo on several occasions and the drugs baron now trusted him more than anyone else under his command.

They caught the first British Airways flight that afternoon from Heathrow, and soon found themselves under the grey leaden skies of Scotland's capital city. It was a miserable dreich sort of day, but quite in tune with their sombre mood since they had serious business to attend to north of the border.

Serrano and Paulo settled into one of the airport bars while they waited for a call from their driver who had been dispatched to pick up a hire car from the nearby Enterprise depot.

Jose Maria had developed a bit of a penchant for Scotch during his last visit to the United Kingdom. So he and Paulo sought out a couple of Glen Ords while they waited for their driver and polished them off in record time. It might not fortify them against the climate in the northern hemisphere, but it was part of their preparation for the job in hand.

No one crossed his syndicate - at any level in the organisation.

Very soon they were en route to a rendezvous at Ocean Terminal in Leith.

-Chapter Forty Seven-

Robert Hayton was a senior civil servant, based at Pacific Quay in Edinburgh and employed by the Scottish Government. His responsibilities included liaison with the UK Government on fiscal matters and working with Scottish local authorities to mitigate some of the adverse effects of the Coalition Government's Welfare Reform Act.

Dubbed the most significant changes to the welfare state since Beveridge, these measures were ostensibly to simplify the benefits regime and change the claimant culture, but mainly to curb the multi-billion pounds cost to the national Exchequer in London that was fast becoming unmanageable.

None of this was part of the plan 70 years ago when William Beveridge wrote the blueprint for the modern welfare state.

"Want is one only of five giants on the road of reconstruction… the others are disease, ignorance, squalor and idleness," he wrote in Social Insurance and Allied Services.

Hayton understood that the policy intention was then and is now to have a simple system to help those who through no fault of their own, cannot fend for themselves. Successive governments, however, had sought to target and restrict entitlement to such an extent that an almost unfathomable and overly complex means-testing regime had evolved. You just had to ask anyone who had the misfortune to apply for assistance. The current political focus was therefore on always "making work pay," and so reducing the so-called dependency culture for all those between 16 and 64 years of age.

Robert walked slowly towards Ocean Terminal, known locally as much for its tourism role, being the last resting place of the Royal Yacht Britannia, as for the adjacent shopping centre that bears its name. He was thinking hard about the right royal row that was brewing within his department. Civil servants are meant to be apolitical, but that doesn't stop them having private opinions, when they think that the politicians in London or Edinburgh are treading perilously close to the edge of a cliff.

There was dissention in the ranks. The UK policy objectives were all very well, but the timescales for introducing the new Universal Credit were unrealistic, systems ill-prepared and above all there was real concern about the "unintended consequences" that would follow for some of the most vulnerable in Scottish society. All of this at a time when the country was in double or maybe triple dip recession. Those who failed to find jobs would find the euphemistically named "conditionality" terms applied and have their family's benefit entitlement significantly reduced. The Government's own recently released figures for their Welfare to Work programme proved that the programme was not yet anywhere near meeting its targets – indeed critics were claiming quite justifiably that better outcomes would have been achieved if the department had sat on its hands and done nothing.

A pessimist, he thought, might echo the words of Kafka, who once said: *"Every revolution evaporates and leaves behind only the slime of a new bureaucracy."*

Robert had not had a good day. His trouble was fundamentally that he too thought that Ministers had chosen the wrong time for such far-reaching changes, the success of which would depend upon increased employment opportunities being generated. Unfortunately the economic climate was wrong, and all that would happen was that some customers would experience delays in receiving their entitlement. Local economies would lose out financially.

Even although he supported the principles of the benefit cap, which meant that those on benefit should not receive more than those in gainful employment, and the social sector size criteria (otherwise known as the spare room subsidy or bedroom tax depending on political persuasion), he knew that the circumstances in high-rented central London that were driving British policy were quite different from those in rural Scotland. In the Highland area, for example, where were the local houses or jobs within reasonable travelling distance to be found for those disadvantaged by the new regime?

The Scottish local authorities and to some extent the Scottish Government would inevitably have to pick up the pieces and do whatever they could by way of mitigation, so the reforms were simply another way of devolving responsibilities and associated costs away from Westminster. "Quelle surprise!"

It is quite a short walk from Pacific Quay to Ocean Terminal. Robert had been asked by his wife to do some minor shopping there before returning home to Cramond. He was still preoccupied, however, with issues of State. Because he had a little time on his hands, he made his way directly to a coffee bar so that he could sit quietly and enter some of his thoughts into the i-Pad that he always carried with him.

After some friendly banter with the young exchange student serving behind the bar, he took his coffee and cream scone to a quiet corner of the lounge, which had full height partitions between groups of seats.

He didn't spot the group of four men seated behind him.

-Chapter Forty Eight-

Serrano was becoming an increasingly worried man. He was fast forming the conclusion that incompetence by his subordinates in the United Kingdom was endangering the European supply chain.

He had been fully briefed by JG's controller on the Loch Lomond incident and the events that had followed, but although that particular and relatively trivial consignment had been retrieved, many loose ends had been left. Any one of these might be sufficient to expose operatives under his command. With careful detective work by the authorities Jose Maria knew that this could lead them in time to himself and even the few faceless men who held the real power in the Cartel.

Serrano's policy of ruthlessness and strategy to root out any weak links in the chain had proved to be quite an effective insurance policy in the past, but he knew that it would only take one informer to spoil the party. He would go from respectable captain of South American industry representing the nation of Colombia to felon overnight.

Of immediate concern to him, was the fact that the sports boat crew on Loch Lomond had eluded his organisation. How much did they know? – It must be something when they had disappeared so completely from view.

Fortescue had disappeared also. He had been known in the past to go on weeklong benders with his friend Big Aggie, but he had been well warned of the consequences of ever doing so again. His last message to JG had been on the way to remote Glen Affric, complete with hostage, so what had befallen him? Serrano feared the worst.

Then there were the bodies that kept appearing – an old fisherman apparently drowned in the loch by Fortescue; also a pillar of the Edinburgh legal establishment tortured beyond endurance in a vain attempt to have him reveal the whereabouts of the Hunters. Either Forbes Mackenzie genuinely did not know or he was an extremely brave man.

Anyway it did not matter now. What was left of him was floating in the Water of Leith.

Such events were unfortunate to say the least. Murders were high profile crimes, attracting additional police resources. Detective work focused upon finding a causal connection. It was all becoming uncomfortably close to home.

Jose Maria, contrary to the reputation that preceded him, was a man of few words. When his two visitors had nervously imparted to him the little knowledge they had about the local situation, he rose quickly to his feet and thanked them for their co-operation.

He then turned to his minder and surreptitiously raised one eyebrow.

Paulo knew what this meant.

-Chapter Forty Nine-

Prisoner 3527398 (Fortescue) in the meantime was being held securely in Porterfield pending charges that included murder, abduction, and being involved in the supply of large quantities of Class A drugs.

He had told all that he knew concerning the activities of the traffickers, but this was not very much due to his lowly status in the organisation. What he did provide was corroboration and an increased level of detail of some facts that were already known to the Constabulary and to SOCA.

His co-operation with the police was for personal advantage rather than through any sense of altruism. It did however extend to participation in a sophisticated sting operation that had been extremely successful, leading not only to the apprehension of JG (or whatever he was now called), but also to vital intelligence regarding an imminent shipment due to be landed upon the Ayrshire coast.

A considerable bonus was that in addition to forged passports and large sums of cash, JG had stupidly retained sufficient evidence hidden in his home to establish a clear link with Serrano's operatives in Colombia and Venezuela.

This was one breakthrough that the international investigation team had long been waiting for.

-Chapter Fifty-

Although his Duck Bay investigations to all intents and purposes had been completed, DS Ramsay had been asked to continue liaising with SOCA and to do what he could to ensure a successful conclusion to the trafficking case.

Strathclyde Police had promised him all necessary resources, including the on-demand availability of an armed response unit. In the circumstances, it was comforting for him to know that serious backup was available.

He was in constant contact too with the Coastguard Service, whose officers were monitoring ship movements on the Clyde, and there was every indication that a drop was only days away.

Customs officers were already in place around the Portencross area, the location on the Ayrshire coast specified by way of the GPS co-ordinates (lat. 53.81, long -4.06) found hidden on the person of JG. He had even been found in possession of a piece of paper with the reference 17538 48921 which one of the investigating team immediately recognised as an Ordnance Survey grid reference that happily agreed with the GPS.

Coincidentally this attractive coastal spot close to Portencross Castle and near West Kilbride was the scene of a murder on October 18th, 1913, described in the Largs and Millport Weekly News of the time as "*a terrible and most mysterious tragedy to the occupants of the lonely cottage of Northbank, which lies immediately under the precipitous cliff of The Three Sisters.*"

The murder as Ramsay knew remains unsolved to this day. The hardened police officer shivered as he walked past the remains of the stone-built traditional cottage, past the very window through which shots were fired at the three occupants, a Mr and Mrs Alexander Maclaren and Mr Maclaren's sister-in-law, Mrs Mary Gunn. Speculation was rife at the time as to the motive behind the killings. Detective work over many years had extended across the pond as far as Canada but to no avail.

One theory that was never taken seriously was that there might be some connection between the cottage's remote location right next to the Firth of Clyde and what befell the tenants.

"History tells us," thought Ramsay "that this was not the first time that violent raiders have been attracted to this very area. After all, the Vikings were in the general location at the time of the Battle of Largs."

"Matters might have been very different about a hundred years ago, if I and my team had been on the case."

The DS also had been reading in his spare time that the neighbouring Portencross Castle has a history going back many hundreds of years and it is a scheduled ancient monument because of this. It was constructed in three phases starting around 1360, but after the 1600s, local fishermen occupied it until the roof was destroyed in a gale in January 1739. Nowadays the waters of the Clyde still come very close to the ruined castle in its

secluded location, not at all far from the Maclarens'
cottage.

The actual village of Portencross had been inhabited for
thousands of years. An archaeological dig found
evidence of an Iron Age settlement dating from 800 to
100BC on Auldhill, just behind Portencross Castle.

All of this information was of little operational use but
very interesting to the policeman as he whiled away the
long hours, waiting from a call from the Coastguard
that would signal the proper start of Operation Viking.

-Chapter Fifty One-

Robert Hayton, the mild-mannered civil servant, had
enjoyed his cappuccino. It made him think less about
the "unintended consequences" of welfare reform.
Perhaps if he had realised the consequences for himself
of choosing that particular coffee bar in Leith at that
specific time of day, he would have saved himself even
more personal grief.

He was unaware of his proximity to Serrano and friends
when he took his seat, but more significantly they had
assumed that they were alone in the bistro. They were
seated in the far corner of the establishment next to the
fire door, and only a bamboo partition separated them
from the lone coffee drinker.

Hayton had thought initially that those at the next table
were tourists. This wasn't an unreasonable conclusion
to come to in view of their swarthy appearances, and
the fact that they seemed to lack the simple courtesies

of those with whom the delicate Hayton was more accustomed to associate.

It was only when they started speaking loudly in Spanish that he began to take a proper interest. He knew from his modern language studies that Spanish is not spoken exclusively in Spain. Statistically there are more Spanish speakers in Mexico and Colombia than there are on the Iberian Peninsula, not to mention a plethora of local dialects.

Gradually he formed the impression that their origin was Central or South American, but beyond that he could not be certain. They were loud and they were aggressive; that much he could tell. And they were up to no good. So much so that Hayton became quite alarmed. He had the presence of mind, however, to surreptitiously press audio record on his i-Pad.

With his wife, he had once attended the local premiere of the latest Bond offering, Skyfall, and secretly fancied himself in the fantasy role. After all he, like 007, was a civil servant, although there the similarity ended.

-Chapter Fifty Two-

When the call eventually came through about Operation Viking, night was already falling and even DS Ramsay's regulation-issue long johns weren't able to stop the "chill of the Clyde" reaching his nether regions.

Perhaps the late comedian Chic Murray could have substituted the word "chill" for "song" in a musical rendition parodying the old standard? He chuckled as he imagined such a performance, and even began to consider how the first few verses might sound. - However, a public rehearsal from a serving police officer that was tone-deaf might provide reasonable grounds for dismissal from the Force, so he kept the new lyrics to himself.

He was mightily relieved to learn that the vessel his Coastguard colleagues were targeting was proceeding in a more southerly direction, which would take it well beyond Portencross, suggesting a rearranged landfall or rendezvous somewhere in North or South Ayrshire.

Perhaps Ramsay might even have time for a sauna in the Seamill Hydro Hotel just up the road, before resuming his duties? ......Now he understood why, in the dim and distant past invaders of Scotland such as the Romans put such a high priority upon constructing their elaborate bath houses and steam rooms, like the one excavated near Bearsden, now in the suburbs of Glasgow less than 30 miles away.

"It was because the climate in the West of Scotland was so insufferably cold!!"

His shift was soon to be at an end, so he handed over formally to another officer and made his way post haste to the warmth of the nearby hotel.

Before long he was ensconced on a leather Chesterfield in front of a blazing log fire, large Single Malt in hand. A regular size Single Malt was too small, and he knew from experience that ordering a double Single Malt was confusing for bar staff even when he, the customer, was stone cold sober. He had rung his wife from the car to let her know that he wouldn't be home, and soon all thoughts of surveillance and wind chill went out of his head as he started to snore.

It was almost midnight when he was gently woken by the buxom barmaid, bending down and asking him:

"Have you no home to go to, Love?"

"Yes," said the policeman, "but I can always stay here with you, Pumpkin."

To his regret his slurred request to her was politely refused, and having wished the remaining clientele a more fulsome goodnight than strictly necessary he made his way slowly to his solitary bedroom, secure in the knowledge that despite the hazards of police work, his marriage to his long-suffering wife of 30 years had survived, to be fought for another day.

-Chapter Fifty Three-

Back in Leith, all this excitement was getting too much
for Hayton. Or maybe it was just the effect of the
(appropriately Colombian) Alta Rica? -Whatever it was
he felt an urgent need to visit the little boy's room.

He stood up, leaving his tablet and coat where they
were, and gingerly made his way around the partition
and towards the loo. He did not look in the direction of
the other customers, but they certainly looked at him.

One of the strangers made his way to the toilet door and
stood impatiently as if waiting for the facilities to be
vacated.

As Hayton came out Serrano's man Paulo seized his
elbow and unexpectedly swung him round. He was
swiftly bundled out the fire exit with his head held
firmly in a vice-like grip before he even had time to
draw breath.

This happened so quickly that it was only at closing time that the waitress noticed Robert's overcoat and iPad lying where he had left them, and the fact that the fire exit door was ajar. His spectacles lay where they had fallen.

Mrs Hayton's groceries would be undelivered that evening. Instead of the planned sirloin steaks for their evening meal, it was Robert's time to be grilled.

The culinary skills had been learned in Bahia de Guantanamo, and no food was involved.

He would be a little late home.

-Chapter Fifty Four-

Full English in the Hydro hotel is a bit of a
contradiction in terms.

"At least the English bit is" thought DS Ramsay, as he
tucked manfully into his breakfast of freshly made
porridge followed by an enormous omelette filled with
local smoked salmon.

He once had a superior officer who in his spare time
was a taster for one of the good food guides. Whereas
his colleague considered himself to be a bit of a
gourmet, Ramsay's own tendencies were more of the
gourmand variety. His fellow officers never failed to
wonder how he managed despite a prodigious appetite,
to remain reasonably in shape.

Having stuffed himself silly " of course, to ensure best
value at all times for his public sector employers," he
helped himself to a second white linen napkin from a
neighbouring table. After wiping his face and hands,

the DS made his way to the hotel reception desk to collect his overnight case and pay his bill. There he was handed a recently received sealed official envelope containing the revised coordinates for his continuing assignment.

As the Customs Officers had thought, the suspect vessel had made course down the Firth of Clyde to Ayrshire and was presently berthed alongside a semi-derelict wharf at Irvine Harbour.

It is a little known fact that the town of Irvine, which first received Royal Burgh status in 1372 from King Robert 11, was for many years the main port in West Central Scotland. A thriving maritime trade and even a shipbuilding industry in Irvine were eclipsed only in the 19th Century by growth in Glasgow, when the River Clyde was eventually dredged. From then on traffic at the Port of Irvine had declined in importance.

Nowadays it is ironic that access to Irvine Harbour from the bay is once again restricted by an old sandbar to boats of relatively shallow draft, and principally to those for leisure use.

Whether by dint of meticulous planning or happy co-incidence, the Captain of the Panamanian-registered Miraflor had waited for high tide and had taken shelter in the little used harbour where under most normal circumstances such a vessel's visit would pass virtually unnoticed.

But these were far from normal circumstances, as the crew were soon to find out.

Operation Viking was re-scheduled for later that weekend.

-Chapter Fifty Five-

Hayton was being held at knifepoint in the back of the rental car as it left Leith and joined the slow evening traffic heading north away from the capital and towards Perth. He was in a state of extreme bewilderment and not a little fear. None of the occupants of the car spoke any English to him as he sat uncomfortably with his hands tightly secured behind his back.

He had managed to translate only a few words of the conversation among his three kidnappers, and the trio's pecking order was very evident to him. The leader in the front passenger seat was throwing his weight about. It was becoming clearer by the moment that whoever they thought Hayton was and whatever they thought he had done, they certainly believed that he was a major thorn in their flesh.

One of the gang was putting forward the proposition that he was a plain-clothes policeman, but another was giving him the benefit of the doubt.

"How much had he overheard of their business in the coffee shop, and was he as harmless as he looked? After all, he had cried like a baby when propelled out of the establishment and into the car, and was already a quivering wreck."

Something about the behaviour of his prisoner eventually convinced Serrano that he was dealing with an innocent abroad, someone caught up in a situation that he neither liked nor understood. In an uncharacteristic gesture, Serrano determined to put a premature end to his misery.

He ordered his driver to stop the vehicle at a quiet spot and had his two associates frogmarch Hayton who, being in a perpetual state of terror could hardly walk, from the road towards an empty children's play park.

What followed next greatly surprised the henchmen.

Instead of the customary beating and swift dispatch that they expected, Serrano came across to where Hayton was seated rather incongruously on a children's slide. He patted the snivelling civil servant on the head, and ignored his pleas for mercy. The prisoner might as well have been talking gibberish to the Colombians for all that they could understand, as indeed he was due to his mental state.

Paulo then produced a hypodermic syringe filled with a milky liquid, with which he quickly injected Hayton in the posterior, and that was that.

He was found in the same position and completely covered by an expensive heavy overcoat the following afternoon, by an unsuspecting young mother taking her children to play on the swings after school.

By this time the perpetrators of the crime expected to have left the country and to be far from Scottish jurisdiction.

Meanwhile, Hayton's poor wife still waited for news of her errand boy.

-Chapter Fifty Six-

Two days later, a male patient in the intensive care unit of Perth Royal Infirmary began to stir. He drifted in and out of consciousness for a period of time and then he was violently sick. He felt as if he was suffering from concussion, but there were no external signs of trauma.

All he knew was that his brain felt as if it were spinning violently within his skull. It didn't matter whether his eyes were open or closed; the awful symptoms were the same. His plight was such that he would happily have accepted euthanasia. His whole body was trembling alarmingly and he had to be restrained, otherwise there was no telling what damage he would do to himself.

He carried no identification on his person and it took twelve hours or so before the delirium had subsided and he was well enough for doctors to decide to ask him his name; quite a long time thereafter for him to be able to reply. This may have been due to the excessive amount of a memory-suppressing drug in his system, a veterinary medication most commonly used to subdue horses.

Eventually the mystery man was able to confirm his name and the town he was born in, but it took the local police quite a long time to piece together just exactly what had befallen him.

As Hayton had been posted as a missing person, it was not too long before his wife, Mildred, was at his side. Even although she was fervently religious, she had almost given up hope of ever seeing her husband alive again.

A long road to recovery lay ahead.

Although physically unharmed, the civil servant's memory loss attributable to the high dosage of the drug that had been administered was quite comprehensive. He did not even recognise Mildred.

-Chapter Fifty Seven-

On board the Miraflor, the sun was well past the yardarm on Sunday but all was still quiet.

The crew were more accustomed to the hustle and bustle of large working ports than they were to the relative peace and quiet of the Ayrshire coast. Most of them were taking advantage of the unusual circumstances by remaining warmly tucked up in their beds. The vodka they had consumed the night before encouraged them in this pursuit although Ramos, the young cook on board, had gone walkabout ashore and despite his poor English had formed a connection with a young lady from the Harbour hostelry. He hadn't returned to the ship the previous evening, but he hadn't even been missed.

Most of his crewmates were equally in the dark as to how long they would be remaining on the Clyde coast. Having been recruited on an open contract and being well paid by international standards for their endeavours, they were content to work from day to day and not to ask too many questions. Only the skipper and the first mate knew the true intentions of those who had chartered the vessel.

The skipper and first mate were taciturn by nature and seen as unapproachable by the seamen. It didn't pay to be too curious in this type of situation.

Their main cargo was described on the manifest as a consignment of salt shipped from the evaporation ponds near Kralendijk on the small island of Bonaire in the Southern Caribbean. There was nothing remarkable in that fact, other than that the crew did not know the cargo's destination. Also the vessel had been loaded at the dedicated pier on Bonaire before any of them had in fact been recruited for the crossing to the United Kingdom.

They were a strange bunch of different nationalities, but all were experienced seamen nevertheless. On the crossing they had pulled together surprisingly well as a team. Ramos thought this was principally due to their fear of the domineering and over-moustachioed Captain, and in deference to his cabinet of modern firearms and ammunition that had been seen hidden in his cabin, rather than to any real sense of loyalty or comradeship.

At about 4pm Ramos and his new lady friend, June, were sauntering back to the wharf at which the Miraflor was berthed (by a strange quirk of fate the very one used many years previously by ICI's Nobel Division to park their "dynamite" or TNT boats), when all Hell broke loose!

-Chapter Fifty Eight-

It was only stun grenades being detonated, but sounded much worse in the still of the Ayrshire Sunday afternoon.

Ramos had scarcely boarded the steep gangway on the port side, before he felt the shock of the blasts. In panic, he caught his left foot on the loose end of a mooring rope and as if in slow motion fell headfirst off the pier. Down into the gap between the vessel and the rough pier timbers.

His lady friend screamed in panic, but had sufficient wits about her to run back to the ship and see what could be done to rescue her companion. Fortunately he was conscious some 15 feet below and just about able to keep himself afloat, although his precarious position between ship and poorly-maintained quay meant that he was in imminent danger - not of drowning or choking from seaweed ingestion, but of being crushed first between the hull of the Miraflor, which was rocking from side to side, and a heavily barnacle-encrusted sea wall.

Suddenly the whole area was swarming with policemen and other uniformed personnel who seemed to have materialised from nowhere.

June could not believe that they had responded so quickly to her desperate cries for help, but then again she did not know that some of the boys in blue had been concealed locally behind what remained of a disused crane, and others in the derelict former harbourmaster's office directly across the street. They were ready to pounce immediately they heard the signal of the first two grenades. If she had not been solely focused in the heat of the moment on rescuing her friend Ramos from where he had fallen, she would have realised that the uniforms concealed body armour. The fact that some men also carried weapons was evident for all to see.

Ramos was probably the only member of the Miraflor's crew not too unhappy to be taken into police custody that day. He had been unceremoniously hauled by boat hook from the oily water, bleeding from a head wound and lacerated by his brush with the barnacles on the way down - to the extent that he wouldn't be comfortable in a sitting position for several days. At least he was alive.

His fellow crewmen had been taken by surprise by the suddenness of the authorities' assault on their ship. All surrendered immediately and were taken into custody, except the two senior officers in respect of whom it later transpired that international arrest warrants had already been issued.

They ran and desperately barricaded themselves inside the Captain's cabin. They used his concealed arsenal to hold out there for about 40 minutes. Resistance however was futile. Very soon they too were in custody after treatment for their wounds in the accident and emergency department of Crosshouse General Hospital, some 7 miles away.

With the ship's crew out of their way DS Ramsay and the HM Customs squad set about gathering the physical evidence to corroborate what they knew so far about the Cartel's activities. It would be a slow and painstaking process but they prayed that their intelligence was correct and that somewhere within the innermost fabric of the Miraflor, a sufficiently impressive haul of narcotics would be found to put some very powerful and dangerous men in jail for a very long time.

It was hoped, of course, that it would not be necessary to sift through every last grain of the ship's cargo of Caribbean salt, but if that was what it took, they might be in Irvine for a very long time.

-Chapter Fifty Nine-

Even the most expensive and sophisticated miniature tracking devices have their limitations. As luck would have it, the one on Serrano's luggage failed at some stage.

"Perhaps it had been spotted, and removed?" "Or perhaps its battery had simply become exhausted?" Either way, it was apparent that the surveillance had been bungled and the authorities had lost him.

The dogged DS Ramsay, however, was still in pursuit. A catalogue of old-fashioned evidence was stacking up with every day that passed.

His attention had been drawn most recently to reports of a flurry of unusual activity in the Edinburgh area, and it certainly wasn't the pandas at Corstorphine Zoo.

The boffins had checked out the Government Issue

i-Pad, retrieved earlier in the week from the Leith coffee bar. They had traced it to the man found semi-conscious in the children's playground. The latest activity on it consisted of an audio file containing men apparently arguing in a foreign language, and it didn't take long for Ramsay to put two and two together. Although the coffee bar had no security camera, the streetwise American student acting as barista on the day of the recording, was able to give a general description of the swarthy men who had left in a hurry leaving half their coffee undrunk and their bill unpaid. Even without CCTV footage, the seasoned detective was convinced that he was on the right trail.

"But how did this senior Government employee fit into the Cartel equation?"

"Surely it was inconceivable that he personally was involved?"

Without any meaningful input from Robert Hayton who by this time was slowly piecing back together some of the pieces of his shattered life and gradually regaining some of his short-term memory, Ramsay found his involvement difficult to understand.

And it was even more incomprehensible when he met Mildred Hayton at the middle-aged gentleman's hospital bedside later that evening.

Ramsay had never met such a gentle and loving couple as the Haytons. They clearly doted on each other and despite Robert's obvious mental impairment, he was most anxious to co-operate with police enquiries. Try as he might, however, he drew a blank and became quite emotional when trying to recall anything about what occurred at Ocean Terminal or in the period leading up to his hospitalisation. Medical staff had never seen such effective drug-induced amnesia, and after about 5 minutes they discouraged Ramsay from asking further questions.

Over a cup of tea, however, the patient's wife did mention Robert's apparently continuing fixation with whatever was on his i-Pad. Whatever it was, it was important enough to keep him awake during the night.

"Was there a connection?"

On his way back to Glasgow the Detective Superintendent used the car phone to ask for an immediate translation of the audio file.

-Chapter Sixty-

Serrano was still in London when he received word of the raid on the Miraflor. Even in his terms the high quality contraband that he knew the ship to contain, was beyond precedent in terms of scale for the European market.

His lieutenants had taken every possible measure and spared no expense to avoid detection. They had twice hermetically-sealed the highest purity product in medical quality polythene, and in turn had encased these parcels in molten plastic from which any remaining air was again withdrawn.

No one involved in the pre-sealing stage was present or touched the sealed product, which was chemically cleaned to remove any trace or smell that might generate a canine response.

Several tons of steel plate had been removed from the ship at its refit in 2007, to permit the fabrication of bespoke storage compartments for the drugs. These he knew to be cunningly welded within the heavy gauge steel of the overhead doors that protected the thousands of tons of legitimate manifest. He personally had signed off the work done to alter the ship, and measures had been taken to ensure the silence of any persons having knowledge of what was done.

Such was the Cartel's confidence in their ability to distribute their drugs around the world in this way that the Miraflor, an elderly vessel that blended in quite easily with other coastal traffic and which had been inspected on numerous occasions, was their vessel of choice when it came to larger consignments. The longer they operated with impunity, the stronger their confidence grew that their illicit trade would remain undetected.

The thought that even now the UK Customs Officers might be tearing his ship apart angered Serrano.

What enraged him even more was the fact that his Captain and some of the crew had apparently put up quite a firefight to prevent the authorities boarding. If the officers on the raid had any doubts as to the veracity of their intelligence about the Miraflor, these would have been dispelled with each and every round of high velocity ammunition that was fired in misplaced loyalty. From the Cartel's perspective the Captain's armoury was to discourage pirates or other thieves – not to outgun the authorities!

Serrano was still personally convinced that the official search would draw a blank and his merchandise would not be found – after all two separate raids in Holland last year had revealed nothing despite over a week of intensive searching.

-Chapter Sixty One-

The Cartel had tentacles everywhere. Even as JG languished in his prison cell, he received a visit from a prison insider whose family had been threatened.

It was in the dead of night when most prisoners in B Wing were asleep, that one of the warders, a slim weasel of a man with thin lips and an unusually pallid complexion, appeared at the door of his cell. JG did not know him from Adam, but was intrigued by what he had to say. He didn't believe a word of it of course, especially the bit about how the Colombians would be prepared to let him live out his life quietly after he had served his 10 year sentence. He knew what had happened to others for lesser misdemeanours.

So what was expected of him to earn their apparent forgiveness? – He had to provide them with information that they so very badly needed. "Any clues however slight, that he had, or had been passed to him by Ted Fortescue, that would help the organisation identify and eventually trace all the occupants of the sports boat; the family who had succeeded in evading the Cartel so far."

JG, like Fortescue knew he had become the architect of his own downfall as soon as he started to co-operate with the police, and suspected that he was already a dead man in the eyes of Serrano, the boss who prided himself in his reputation for tying up the loose ends.

Information received by the Cartel indicated that all members of the Hunter family had disappeared from sight, and this suggested a Witness Protection involvement.

"They surely wouldn't have stepped in unless the family were in possession of evidence that would be of value to the prosecution in any future case?"

The warder gave JG until breakfast time next morning to think of his response. He had plenty of time to do so, because he never slept a wink for the rest of that night.

When the morning came, his bedclothes were screwed up on the floor.

His appearance evoked memories of the Wreck of the Hesperus but at least he had made up his mind.

-Chapter Sixty Two-

On its own, the transcript of the recording from the i-Pad did not constitute sufficient evidence to implicate Serrano in any Cartel activities. What it did confirm to Ramsay was that the Colombian was undoubtedly calling the shots when it came to the coercion and manipulation of his associates.

It was clear from the translation that he had instigated the kidnapping of Hayton on the spur of the moment, because he was fearful of what he might have heard, and he was determined above all to protect his (unspecified) business interests from damaging disclosures.

What the detective could not initially understand was why someone so meticulous in other matters could have failed to spot the i-Pad that had been left behind in Leith.

Further checking revealed that the credit for this would have to be given to Hayton himself who it appears had discreetly covered the tablet by a napkin before visiting the gents' toilet.

Over a period of a week or so, surveillance personnel had separately accumulated quite a catalogue of photographs featuring the Colombians and their British associates.

The Detective Superintendent and his SOCA colleagues were now part of a large international team fast closing in on this particular Cartel, and Ramsay knew that although Serrano was technically off his patch, English colleagues were once again tracking his whereabouts. Every small piece of the jigsaw puzzle would be useful as evidence in due course.

-Chapter Sixty Three-

Sarah Mackenzie, as all her friends know is a strong-willed young lady who does not take kindly to being told what to do.

It had been bad enough losing her father in such dramatic and harrowing circumstances, and being told by the police that she would not be permitted for her own safety to return to the New Town, but when the old judge's body was eventually released for burial and it was recommended she postpone any ceremony, that was the final straw.

The great and good of the capital city were expecting a funeral befitting someone of Forbes' rank, and she would see that they were not disappointed. A fulsome obituary had already appeared in the Scotsman, ironically spelling out some of the celebrated criminal cases over which the judge had presided, but it was the circumstances of his cruel death that made the headlines.

It seemed to his daughter that what the tabloid press didn't know, they made up. One daily newspaper, for example had serialised what they knew of the events leading up to his torture on the cellar floor in Leith. They assumed, not unreasonably that this was all in retaliation for the draconian sentences that he had imposed on some of the High Court's finest, but how wrong they were. Fact is often stranger than fiction.

Another even had a lurid and embellished account of her father's evening out with his legal cronies in the Rose Street area, courtesy of his cab driver.

-Chapter Sixty Four-

On the day of the funeral, only Sarah was allowed to attend. It was considered much too dangerous for Fraser who was still a marked man, so brave Sarah cut a lonely but attractive figure in black lace and deliberately-chosen extra high heels as she elegantly negotiated the cobbles and slowly followed her father's mahogany coffin into St Giles.

There were about 300 in the congregation, slightly more than she had expected. - What she didn't know was that within the serried ranks of mourners were several armed police officers, and even more worryingly some representatives of the criminal fraternity.

"How many of the mourners," she thought, "were real friends - ten per cent or perhaps less?" Sarah would dearly have loved to know who all the people were, if nothing else but to learn a little bit more about her devoted but somewhat eccentric father. It was too late now to understand what really made him tick, and whether all that exposure to the seedier side of life had rubbed off at all on him. She didn't think so.

"Perhaps that was due in no small measure to his faith in the insulating and oxidising properties of fine red Burgundies?"

All eyes were on her later as she stepped graciously forward at the end of the Church of Scotland service, placed her gloved hand fondly and tenderly on the coffin and then slowly wiped away a tear.

Forbes had chosen the hymns himself some years previously when he had a health scare, but there were many present that day who thought that "Fight the Good Fight" was particularly appropriate.

Sarah herself was whisked away at the conclusion of the service and before the other members of the congregation were permitted to leave. Her escort was an experienced police driver who had been detailed to protect her and ensure her safe return to Fraser at a new secure address some 20 miles away. They were taking no chances. A second unmarked police vehicle was deployed to effect a temporary road closure in order to make certain that they were not followed when they left the Cathedral.

In the back row, DS Ramsay uttered a sigh of relief and slid quickly along to the end of the pew. In doing so he tore his trousers and hurt himself on a splinter of wood. Apart from this affront to his dignity he was satisfied that the service had gone without incident, but he had continuing concerns about keeping the Hunters and their immediate contacts (now including Sarah) safe and well hidden, until at least the Miraflor's illicit cargo had been located and seized.

-Chapter Sixty Five-

Jose Maria was surprisingly well read for someone who had pulled himself up by the bootstraps. For much of his adult life he never travelled anywhere without a newspaper or book to read, and he had largely educated himself through the printed word. He felt it gave him the edge in negotiations. "What else would explain his personal track record, and meteoric rise in his chosen line of business?"

Only the previous evening he had opened his Kindle (he had bought one of the first) in the comfort of the piano lounge of his Kensington hotel. He was reading a biography of General Douglas MacArthur, Chief of Staff of the United States Army during the 1930s and someone who played such a prominent role in the Pacific theatre during World War II.

Serrano admired the single-minded and business-like manner in which the old soldier had devised battleground strategy and motivated his subordinates over a long and distinguished military career. Although from different worlds, the Colombian identified very closely with the sentiments of the much-decorated officer. Serrano's ego was such that he even went so far as to consider himself MacArthur's equal in many respects.

The next morning he remembered one quotation in particular that had been attributed to MacArthur:

"No matter how extreme a situation appears at first, it is never as bad or as good as it at first appears."

How appropriate therefore, that this particular gem of philosophy was in the forefront of Jose Maria's mind when his iPhone rang unexpectedly.

"Ola?"

To his surprise it was an international call from a trusted associate in Venezuela, someone employed in the upper reaches of law enforcement, but very much more gainfully employed in the service of the Cartel. His speciality was encryption and covert communications.

Serrano's cigar-stained fingers played nervously with the ends of his black moustache as he considered the import of the call. His cold steely grey eyes and furrowed brows said it all. Nothing was communicated in response, but he would now need some considerable time to consider his options.

The information relayed to him was serious. So serious that had he been a General like MacArthur in charge of many battalions of battle-weary troops, he would have had no alternative but to rethink his entire battlefield strategy, and perhaps his career. No amount of philosophical gymnastics would make him feel better. He exhaled slowly as if drawing his last breath.

And what momentous piece of information conspired to ruin his evening and shatter his peace of mind?

– Simply a realisation that the search of the Miraflor had after all, and contrary to his confident expectations, revealed his entire European stash.

-Chapter Sixty Six-

Serrano was on the horns of a dilemma.

His first inclination was to flee the country. He would have done so long ago, but to alter his business schedule now would be tantamount to an admission of guilt. He suspected that his every move was already being scrutinised, and even if that were not the case the authorities would almost certainly have put a watch on all ports and airports.

To leave now, or even to try to leave when his published schedule, as a respectable businessman carrying out industrial and commercial visits as part of a trade mission, was public knowledge - would be a big mistake.

And so he stayed.

His programme for the next seven days entailed trips to factories in the Midlands and the North East, and he knew that these would try his patience. Colombian Civil Servants supported him in these visits.

Even in the good times, when his mind was clear of Cartel issues, he remembered thinking that he would rather be anywhere else than in the gloom of post-industrial England. His fellow countrymen might be poor, but at least they managed the occasional smile. His immediate entourage also had enough money to enjoy themselves, even if others had to pay the price for their extravagances.

"Were they and he happy? "- He couldn't quite answer that one now, even for himself.

His family's lifestyle was certainly in the upper echelons. They mixed internationally with some of the rich and famous, but he himself always felt slightly ill at ease. He hardly had a sunny personality. It was almost as if he quietly knew in the depths of his soul, or what was left of it, that money was only one facet of what was necessary for happiness.

Even his very own Luz Marina had been happy in her days treading the Teatro boards. Replacing her costume jewellery with pieces by Cartier had won her over in the beginning, but she now knew him too well. She maybe now knew how apply the "5 Cs test" to valuing diamonds, but her husband's wealth and power came at a heavy price - the price of intimidation and raw fear that affected all in his immediate circle.

If she was in any doubt about that, she was reminded on a daily basis by the loaded weapon that shared their bed every night, and the nightly ritual at home of ensuring that all their security doors were bolted and intruder alarms set.

Subconsciously Jose Maria always knew that he didn't belong "upstairs." She knew it too and that he would cling on if necessary by his fingertips, if that meant that he would have a trophy wife on his arm and two Porsches in his garage (not necessarily in that order).

The ham at the top of his particular greasy pole was just too desirable to be ignored. As a poor youngster, he had scaled the dizzy heights at many a local festival and crashed to the ground more than once before. This time he might not be a lean and hungry young gymnast but he could afford spikes in his shoes, so he would persevere.

His gritty determination meant that he had the edge to compete and to survive the worst that the world could throw in his direction. He genuinely believed that he was the one to take home the joint of ham.

" After all, even his name was Serrano."

-Chapter Sixty Seven-

DS Ramsay allowed himself a brief smirk of satisfaction to the press that British officers had succeeded where others such as the Dutch and Belgians had failed. He was responding, of course, to the news that the heavy cargo doors of the Miraflor had given up their substantial secret. Never before had the Port of Irvine played such a hugely important role in the fight against international crime.

And he, Detective Superintendent Iain Mackay Ramsay, had been in the thick of it. This must be the pinnacle of his career. He was involved in the subsequent press conference in the appropriately named Magnum Centre just yards from where the Miraflor was still berthed.

Announcing the good news to the international media made all the cold years on the beat and dealing with the minnows in his various patches of Strathclyde fade into insignificance.

The imperturbable senior officers of the UK Border Agency could not fail to be impressed by the Irvine haul – 1.3 tonnes of 90% pure cocaine. It was the UK's biggest ever Class A drugs seizure, only slightly heavier even than the 1.2 tonnes found in a pleasure cruiser in Southampton in June 2011 – but that had been destined for the Netherlands market.

Since the average purity at the UK border is seldom much over 60%, the street value of the Miraflor consignment after cutting would probably have exceeded £350m. That is roughly equivalent to about one third of the requirement for the whole UK market in any year.

This was the big one, the fish that didn't get away. - Seizure of such a vast quantity of top quality drug was almost beyond comprehension, and he understood only too clearly how many lives would now be saved in the United Kingdom by the remarkable success of the joint enforcement operation.

Ramsay allowed himself another quiet smile of satisfaction to the assembled television cameras, and didn't mind who saw it.

And so it was back to the Ops Room at Pitt Street with his credibility intact, the net rapidly closing in on the perpetrators, and a more generous budget now available from the powers that be, to be spent on whatever was necessary to pursue several clear and developing lines of enquiry.

As a child he had been quite fanatical about doing ever more complicated jigsaws. This one was for real but multi-dimensional, and with his SOCA and international colleagues he could start to visualise the picture that was steadily taking shape before his eyes.

"Timing is everything," said a slightly tipsy Ramsay later as he was briefing his men. "Ask any good comedian! Not that there is anything remotely funny about this lot, but we'll use the old Lobster Pot technique – Once we have got hold of them, we won't be letting them go."

"He's a funny old sod," said his DI after the team had been dismissed. "To continue the lobster analogy, it makes a nice change to see him flushed with success and with his tail up for once."

"If Ramsay had his way, it would be the pushers that would end up being boiled alive, rather than the crustaceans!"

-Chapter Sixty Eight-

It is still a mystery to the police, how the Cartel made the connection between the Hunters and the middle-aged couple returning suntanned to Britain after their sojourn of several months in France, supposedly learning all about the champagne industry. But make the connection they did, and they were even kind enough to send a car for the pair when the 9pm ferry from Rotterdam to Hull docked as usual one Friday evening!

The Hunters had been comprehensively hoodwinked by a bogus communication purporting to be from the Witness Protection Programme. The couple received the official-looking email earlier in the week, informing them that the danger level to their persons had reduced and it was now safe for them to return temporarily to the United Kingdom. As a precaution, they were advised not to contact any family members meantime, or any other police contacts, but to make their way to

Rotterdam where they should return their hire car at the ferry terminal, pick up their prepaid tickets and directly board the channel ferry. They would be met at the other side.

Perhaps it was a triumph of hope over expectation, but the exiles were so relieved to hear the message they had longed for, that they fell for the deception.

When they were met in the UK terminal's arrival area by two smart looking men holding a board with the name Henderson, they greeted them without suspicion and made their way outside as directed, to a green Volvo Estate Car. After the men had loaded their luggage they settled down in the back of the vehicle for what they assumed would be the long journey north.

Before long they were both snoozing, feeling the effects of one too many cognacs they had enjoyed in the ferry bar on the way across, and confident in the knowledge that they were in safe hands.

Had they been more alert they would swiftly have realised that they were being driven in an entirely different direction to what they should have expected.

-Chapter Sixty Nine-

The Volvo headed directly south on the Great North Road.

David woke up at one point and queried where they were heading, but he was palmed off with the response "We have been asked to make a diversion en route for operational reasons." Tired as they were, the couple accepted this explanation although they weren't terribly happy at what seemed to be a very long and inconvenient detour.

The hour or so that followed, was uneventful. It was already after midnight and the two front seat passengers who had pronounced Geordie accents didn't appear to be the most engaging or talkative of individuals. The driver, Bill, was a man in his forties who looked as if he was in need of a good feed. His colleague, who was younger, had the opposite problem. David noted that in the first hour or so of the journey he nervously stuffed his face with bag after bag of chocolate peanuts. He wasn't the sharing type.

Somewhere south of Biggleswade a blue flashing light appeared in the driver's rear view mirror. There was nothing strange about that, but when two more police vehicles took up station beside and in front of their car, the rear seat occupants realised that something was afoot.

Bill's reaction was one of panic. He pressed his accelerator hard to the floor, and narrowly avoided collision with the vehicle in the offside lane. Then, with tyres smoking he threw his car wildly from side to side, attempting to put some distance and other vehicles between himself and the pursuing police officers. They didn't manage to hem him in because the heavy traffic would have made this manoeuvre dangerous for other road users. Instead they put in place a well-rehearsed series of remote actions that would have a similar effect.

"Shut it!" yelled the fat man when the Hunters who by this time were in fear of their lives, started to shout at them. "Do exactly as you are told, or you will die."

He said it as if he meant it, so they complied.

Up ahead the traffic started to slow. The Volvo had no option but to slow down also. David and Louise looked knowingly at each other, unclipped their seatbelts and reached simultaneously for the door handles.

Needless to say, they were child-locked. They were hemmed in.

The cars and lorries ahead started to move again. As the pace increased, Bill zigzagged again from lane to lane, sometimes reaching speeds of ninety miles per hour or higher. His companion in crime by this time was sincerely regretting having eaten so many chocolate peanuts as the car was thrown about.

Far ahead they could see that the traffic was much clearer but suddenly a road roller with yellow indicators flashing was blocking the nearside carriageway. The outer lane was clear.

Bill pressed on, oblivious to a 40mph speed restriction and desperate to escape.

There was a bend to the right. They rounded it at high speed. Only at the last second did the driver realise that the game was up. A hastily laid stinger had noisily punctured all four of the Volvo's tyres. After slewing dangerously to the left and making fairly substantial contact with a crash barrier, it was going nowhere. The Hunters, who were no longer wearing their seatbelts, were only prevented from ending up in the front of the car by the headrests of the seats in front. Airbags had deployed upon impact.

To make matters worse for the two Geordies, they were shocked to see armed police officers in position, their torches and weapons already trained on them. Unwilling to pay the ultimate penalty for the Cartel, they slowly raised their hands in the air.

The kidnap victims were quickly released from the vehicle. In their dazed condition they stumbled out, still not fully understanding what had happened to them.

In a few minutes the officer in charge explained and soon he was reporting the night's developments to DS Ramsay. He was relieved to learn that the Hunters were safe once again. This was thanks mainly to the professionalism and speedy co-operation of the Border Agency staff that had been routinely monitoring traffic from Rotterdam.

"So much for the security of the Witness Protection Programme" thought Ramsay, who knew that his superiors would soon initiate an enquiry at the highest level.

Later that day the two would be re-billeted under the Programme, and this time there could be no mistakes.

-Chapter Seventy-

One of the problems with police work, like all tiers of government is the monotony of the paper chase, the bureaucratic bundles of joy that you ignore at your peril.

Ramsay hated the prescribed tasks every bit as much as his colleagues did. But not for him the paperless office promised by the so-called digital revolution. He had never mastered the skills of the keyboard. He didn't know his PDF files from his MP3, or his tablet from his phablet. - At least this was the impression he liked to give, and he had more of a sense of humour than most colleagues gave him credit for.

He had a long-held conviction that "Someone on my salary should not have to spend any of my valuable time typing," and the seasoned cop never missed a chance to expound upon this theory.

As he had announced to all and sundry at the annual Police Ball, after a particularly dire stage performance of New York, New York:

"If God had meant me to be a real detective, I wouldn't be standing here before you now - paid as a typist, wearing my lipstick, hair extensions, tight fitting lycra mini skirt, push-up bra and high heels."

The alcohol-fuelled audience roared with laughter at the picture he had painted, but the Chief Constable winced, and at least one cross-dresser in the audience of worldly-wise policemen was seen to blush most uncomfortably.

In spite of his prejudices, however, Iain Ramsay got things done. Old-fashioned he might be, but his paper chases told a story.

In the case of Jose Maria Serrano and Associates he was confident that he had amassed so much detailed and meticulously cross-referenced evidence that the case for the prosecution would be more watertight than the hull on the Hunters' sports boat – before Fortescue had messed with it.

-Chapter Seventy One-

Ramsay's domestic circumstances were scarcely the stuff of legend. He lived modestly in the country, even kept a dozen or so chickens in the garden, and in sharp contrast to his professional life liked nothing better than to escape whenever he could from the noise and confusion of the helter-skelter that was everyday police work.

He detested open plan offices, and even more so the latest fashion for hot-desking or the euphemistically named office rationalisation. If the intention really was to save large amounts of money on accommodation costs across the organisation that would be reinvested in fighting street crime, he could see the point of it. From the Superintendent's perspective that just wasn't happening.

Making allowance on any given day for only seven out of ten officers to have a place to park their bottoms in his section was a bit below the belt. Nothing caused him more irritation, except perhaps the never-ending edicts from higher ranks that he should grapple increasingly frustratingly with their inadequately specified information technology systems.

In the Utopian future promised by Mobile and Flexible Working theory it would be appropriate for his whizz kid successors to float between home and office, working effortlessly as they stood at what Ramsay disparagingly called "coffee or kitchen counters" on portable digital devices.

These young bucks like those in Stock Exchanges and in similar establishments around the world would be earning so much that they would not mind a bit of discomfort. It would be good for them and represent excellent training for standing at the champagne and tapas bars in the evenings!

The conventional wisdom, of course, would be that it is not good for individual members of staff to be sedentary for too long. Such an approach would also be helpful to the effectiveness and efficiency of the business by engendering a "staff race to work" in the early morning, in an unsubtle response to competition for the limited number of "battery hen stations" that were available.

Ramsay disagreed fundamentally with the proposition that he and other officers of his rank should show an example to his subordinates and give up their cellular offices.

That was why he was careful to lock his personal office as he left one Friday evening for a spot of well-earned leave.

The sign featuring Salmo Salar that he hung on the outside of the door said it all. He had gone to the River Stinchar!

The Detective Superintendent's knowledge of the wild and anadromous North Atlantic Salmon was considerable. He knew that having been born in fresh water, it migrates to the ocean but returns to the same fresh water to spawn. Research has shown that its precise homing behaviour is a product of highly developed olfactory memory.

"In other words," thought Ramsay, chuckling quietly to himself, "like any good detective, it has a keen sense of smell."

-Chapter Seventy Two-

DI Turner, much to his personal surprise was still attached to the wider Duckbay/Miraflor enquiry. Being a single man and able to relocate relatively easily, his name had quickly come to the fore when additional resources had to be deployed in London on surveillance. He could also hit the ground running because of his prior knowledge of the case, and it avoided briefing a new officer.

That was why he found himself in the unusual position of being a Strathclyde detective peremptorily ordered on to the patch of the Metropolitan Police, and still working closely with the suits in SOCA.

It was now early July. The capital was thronging with tourists many of whom seemed to be making their way to SE19 and the gladiatorial pit that is Wimbledon. Turner had received (source undisclosed) information that a party of Colombian nationals had managed to obtain a small number of Centre Court tickets for the

Wednesday, and that Serrano's wife would be among them.

It had taken a lot of persuasion to obtain a seat close to the visitors (people will go to unbelievable lengths when it comes to the Centre Court), but although his targets' seats were quite far up and did not have a particularly close view of the action, Turner resplendent in tartan shorts and saltire cap would see their every move.

He would be sitting immediately behind them, noting carefully everything that was said. That would not be easy for someone whose lifetime exposure to Spanish was limited to being able to order "dos Cuba Libres" at a beachside bar, but the wire he carried was expected to help in that regard.

Being a poor boy from Inverclyde, Turner had never been to Wimbledon. He scarcely knew the rules of the game and seeing how the other half live was quite an eye-opener.

He had been told that Luz Marina was a bit of a stunner, and spotted her over-the-top designer gear and décolletage immediately as the foreign party took their seats. He would have choked on the strawberries and cream that are de rigueur on Centre Court if he could have afforded any.

Turner was delighted to see that on Court for a place in the 2013 Semi Final was his compatriot from Dunblane and Olympic Gold Medal Winner, Andy Murray, against a lower-ranked Spanish opponent named Fernando Verdasco.

The match was a noisy one with about 15,000 spectators following every hit of the ball and rising to their feet at every opportunity as the talented Scot resisted the difficult left-handed serve and huge forehand of his opponent. Every point was chased. In an amazingly physical game it took quite a while for a relieved Murray to regain his composure and eventually prevail with a final score of 4-6,3-6,6-1,6-4,7-5.

DI Turner, it is fair to say enjoyed his visit to the All England Tennis Club. Even the Colombian party had appeared animated at times as the fortunes of their Spanish favourite had ebbed and flowed. But the Scot had overcome their favourite, and although Turner wasn't to know it Murray would go on to become the Wimbledon Champion, the first Briton since Fred Perry to do so.

Turner didn't think that he had overheard anything of particular importance to the police enquiry. In a large crowd watching such an exciting game of tennis it was difficult to hear anything at all, but he would only know that for sure when his MP3 file was sent for analysis.

-Chapter Seventy Three-

Iain Ramsay was not one to take chances. He would never pass a case to his superiors unless all i's were dotted and the t's crossed. Such was his aversion to risk that his submissions to the Fiscal needed to be as complete and accurate as possible. It was not just a matter of professional detail. It went much further than that.

The DS took a personal pride in the exacting standards that he followed. He was known for his capacity to switch off from everything and anyone when he was on a case, and he had been accused of rudeness to fellow officers on more than one such occasion. He really didn't care. His office door was important to him since the barrier it created allowed him peace to marshal his thoughts and put the world to rights.

He wasn't sure whether he was taciturn by nature, or the job had made him what he now was. His wife considered the latter to be true since she had told him on many occasions that she would never have married a policeman if she had known in advance what the job would do to his personality. His world had polarised into right and wrong, black and white, and there were seldom any shades of grey.

He generally kept his own counsel, speaking only when spoken to and often appearing quite uncommunicative. He only really relaxed with a dram in his hand. As a consequence, Mrs Ramsay had learned long ago that she too was married to the force, and this led to many a domestic confrontation. Her personal solution was to banish the blues, not with alcohol, although she would be the first to admit that she was quite partial to a nice wee glass of Pinot Grigio or Sauvignon Blanc, but with a shopping spree in Glasgow or Edinburgh.

On a superficial level this made her feel better. To see the look on her husband's face as she returned home by taxi with several A-list purchases, cheered her up no end - as well as providing suitable recompense from her husband for services rendered.

All of these thoughts, however, were banished from Ramsay's consciousness as he sat on the bank of the

River Stinchar and played his second fish. He had chosen the Almont Beat because it is one of the most productive on the Ayrshire salmon rivers and has excellent fly water. He knew that the Stinchar was a typical west coast spate river, fishing at its best in falling water immediately after a summer or autumn spate – but Ramsay liked it because in spite of stories of poor catches on other rivers, he had never come away empty-handed on any previous visit.

Safely in the custody of his keep net at the water's edge was already a handsome four-pound salmon – not bad for an hour's work using a hand-tied fly. Iain Ramsay had imbibed one or two celebratory drams from his silver hip flask to welcome his catch, and was feeling quite mellow as he studied the glistening scales on the even heavier fish that was just about to join its companion.

To Ramsay, nothing could compare to the thrill of the chase for a wild and free salmon taken on the rod; not for him the puny chemical-fed versions now farmed in such profusion around the Scottish and Norwegian coasts. It was a bit like comparing his free-range eggs with those from their battery hen equivalents, and they had no fun at all.

As the sun descended to the horizon, Ramsay put down his salmon rod, polished off his second pork pie of the day and drained his hip flask. The warm glow of the Highland Park tasted even better than usual, and before long he was snoozing contentedly in his favourite corner of Ayrshire, dreaming of a life beyond work to escape the frustrations of everyday life in what shortly would become a new and enlarged organisation known as Police Scotland.

-Chapter Seventy Four-

Settled comfortably in the heather, Iain Ramsay slept
for a good couple of hours. At about seven o'clock,
however, a slight breeze lowered the temperature and
try as he might he was forced to leave his reverie.

He dismantled his precious Shakespeare fly rod,
gathered his gear together and stowed it hurriedly with
his catch and all his bits and pieces. He was already late
for his lift from a fellow fisher back into Ayr, so wasted
no time in making his way to the pre-arranged pick up
point on the nearby A714.

Mrs Ramsay in due course met him off the 9pm train
from Ayr at Troon railway station, and the pair of them
drove the short distance to the Lochan House Hotel,
overlooking a fairway on one of the three courses of
Royal Troon Golf Club, formed in 1878 and famous
across the world for hosting the Open Golf
Tournament. The hotel was a long-term family
favourite, and although expensive, even the

parsimonious Ramsay had agreed that the price was justified on this occasion. It was certainly a lot less expensive than it would be in 2016, when Troon was next due to host the Championship.

Manicured lawns led from the guests' carpark past a stone water feature to the hotel entrance, and the couple paused there only for a moment, quite entranced by the antics of a photogenic little three year old in a red and dark blue dress, whose father and mother were asking her to pose beside the fountain.

A polite concierge duly welcomed the couple in the main hallway and arranged for their luggage to be whisked away. They next saw this in their comfortable bedroom after they had completed the usual check-in formalities at the reception desk.

The Ramsays had been allocated the Arran suite on the first floor for the duration of their short stay, and it came as a very pleasant surprise to be upgraded since none of the other rooms had such a splendid view across the Firth of Clyde to the Isle of Arran. Even a basic room was probably at the top end of their family budget. The bottle of chilled Prosecco in the ice bucket at the end of the bed was also most acceptable.

"It's what the doctor ordered," said Iain as he admired his new surroundings, noting that the bathroom alone with its giant freestanding enamel bath in the centre exceeded the size of their master bedroom back at home.

"I'll just pop down to the hotel kitchen and ask them to freeze my catch for me, and then I'll have a hot shower. We can have dinner in our suite tonight as a treat."

With that he jauntily picked up his fishing bag from beside his wife's chair, gave her the obligatory peck on the cheek, and left the room.

It was fully half an hour before he returned, and when he did he was ashen-faced.

"For God's sake, Iain… What is wrong? What has happened?"

It took several minutes before Ramsay could compose himself sufficiently to reply. When he did so, his voice was shaking and the senior police officer couldn't keep his hands from trembling.

Beads of perspiration had appeared on his forehead.

Whether it was fear or emotion, or just far too much John Barleycorn, his long-suffering wife could not yet tell. His complexion was pretty pallid at the best of times.

"Fish finger" she thought he had said, but she couldn't be sure.

-Chapter Seventy Five-

Within 20 minutes the sound of two police cars drawing up outside the hotel interrupted the quietness of the evening. Those residents of the hotel who had already retired for the night – it catered mainly for clientele of a certain age –were surprised to see blue lights flashing and hear the sound of size-ten footwear on the gravel path outside.

The persons concerned seemed to be making their way to the large and well-appointed kitchen at the rear of the premises. The hotel management were fiercely proud of this pristine and largely stainless steel kitchen within which they prepared their award-winning haute cuisine. So much so that they encouraged paying guests to drop in for an inspection or cooking demonstration from time to time.

But not on this occasion!

All the usual activity by chefs and serving staff had ceased, and restaurant employees sent home for the night. There wasn't a waitress now to be seen, and for good reason. Two uniformed officers stood guard at the door, and two gentlemen in suits were interviewing the sous chef.

Open before them on the stainless steel counter next to the fresh lobster holding tank, was Iain's dark olive canvas Royalty Game Bag.

Visible in one of the internal zipped pockets could be clearly seen the larger of his catches for the day. There was nothing remarkable about that.

Except that from the salmon's mouth poked the unmistakeable shape of a severed human finger, the middle digit of someone's right hand…

-Chapter Seventy Six-

One of the hazards of the job, as Ramsay knew only too well was the vulnerability of individual officers.

"How in God's name had anyone got close enough to him to deliver the offending digit?" "What foul brain had thought up such a sickening warning, and for what purpose?"

By the time the DS had recovered his composure, and more importantly had managed to calm down his wife, neither of them felt like eating dinner that evening.

A uniformed police officer was on duty outside their hotel door, and another in the foyer of the hotel, but all of this was far too close for comfort. Ramsay knew that if the Cartel wanted him dead, they had the resources, the muscle and the means to accomplish this without too much difficulty.

On the basis of that day's evidence, they had also had the opportunity. They had managed to get sufficiently near to his fishing bag to leave their calling card – and the bag had been close beside him all day.

Ramsay remembered that he had snoozed in the heather from about 5pm after bagging his catch. He shivered at the thought that someone must have crept up beside him as he slept. "Why," he wondered "had he been spared, and simply warned off, when they (whoever they were) had the opportunity in that remote spot, to quickly slit his throat with every chance of getting away with it?"

"Did they have an ulterior motive in keeping him alive, and for what?"

He had been on the one case for so long now that he believed that only Serrano and his henchmen would know.

Forensics would do their job, but this would only take their enquiries so far.

-Chapter Seventy Seven-

Strange as it may seem to some, Serrano had chosen to stay on in Scotland even although some of his entourage including Paulo had flown back to base in Bogota.

His motives for staying were not clear to the police.

"Was he trying to retrieve what he could of his empire after the Miraflor fiasco, and had he further nefarious deeds to do? Was it all simply camouflage, the arrogant posturing of someone who could already smell the stench of a Colombian or United States gaol? Or had he been tipped off that he would be detained if he chanced his arm and tried to use any of the normal channels to flee the United Kingdom?"

Whichever way it was, the authorities were content to continue surveillance from a distance while international colleagues were piecing together the remaining bits of the jigsaw that would eventually bring his career and liberty to an end.

Local man Ramsay was a thorn in his flesh, the focus of his current pain. Of that there was no doubt, but the boy from the back streets of Bucaramanga had met his likes before.

In retrospect, Ramsay had been foolish to participate in the high visibility Magnum press conference, and Serrano knew that he already would be ruing the day.

The self-important Jose Maria strutted the world stage with delusions of grandeur and a self-belief second to no one, barring perhaps Donald Trump in the USA. - Like Trump he could not afford to fail. His ego would not permit it.

For as long as the Colombian thought he had to remain in the UK he was determined to make the most of his stay, playing the part of a wealthy tourist; and with Luz Marina by his side, staying from week to week in a variety of exclusive hotels.

They both made full use of the country's best hotel facilities from Perthshire to the Scottish Borders, with the Colombian's wife treating herself to several expensive spa treatments, while the man himself invariably had a solitary round of golf nearby, giving him time alone in the great outdoors to consider his next move.

Meanwhile, even as Serrano plotted further torment for the Detective Superintendent who had so badly wronged him, the evidence in the Colombian's personal file mounted day by day.

There had also been dark hints of insubordination across the Pond, but Paulo had his instructions.

-Chapter Seventy Eight-

DI Turner was still on the case, and watching the Colombians from a safe distance. Even although he had been within touching distance of them at Wimbledon in July, he was confident they would not recognise him.

One significant piece of surprising information gleaned from his recording of an animated conversation between Jose Maria and his wife at the tennis, was that plans were afoot for the two of them to have a week's sailing on the west coast. The yacht they were to charter from Largs Marina was relatively modest, and at 44 feet would be much less ostentatious than Serrano's home-based vessel that was used for both business and pleasure.

Nowadays, many sailors still give the Colombian coast a really wide berth with insurance companies imposing surcharges for being in these waters. This is because over the years, there has always been a high risk of attacks on cruising vessels from any one of the 4 main Cartels led by powerful men such as Pablo Escobar.

The scale of activity by the Cartels was staggering. By the early 1990s Escobar alone had amassed a fortune of $30bn. By the time of his violent death in December 1993 at the age of only 44, this figure grew to approximately $100bn if all of his many hiding places across Colombia and elsewhere were taken into account.

The Panama Cruising Guide confirms that in the 1980s and '90s Colombia definitely had major problems with guerrilla groups on the left and the right that kept prudent sailors far from its shores. But after a decade of serious effort, and with US support, Colombia became more stable with "la violenza" reduced to levels typical of other South American countries.

Criminal problems with narco' spin-off gangs of former guerrilleros do continue, but only in very specific regions; for Caribbean cruisers the one area that warrants caution is the bottom of the Gulf of Uraba, a long narrow inlet located on the coast of the country, close to the connection of the continent to the Isthmus of Panama.

This was where Serrano learned to sail.

The Firth of Clyde would be a doddle.

-Chapter Seventy Nine-

As Jose Maria and Luz Marina boarded their tender
and leisurely rowed out the short distance to where
their chartered yacht was moored, the sun was
beginning to set in the west beyond the bold
silhouette that is the Isle of Arran.

It was the kind of glorious crimson evening for
which the Scottish Tourist Board would gladly have
paid good money from their limited marketing
budget.

The boat was a Bavaria 44, 13.7m long and with a
draft of 2.1m. With a beam of 4.39m it had a
comfortable main saloon, more than adequate for
the couple's needs; and central heating to their
cabin, which was considered essential by Luz
Marina. From Jose Maria's point of view, he was
more concerned about the technical side, noting that
there were twin steering positions and a useful bow
thruster; and ensuring that there was a full package

of electronic instrumentation including a chart plotter, complete with instructions for use in his native language.

The 75hp inboard engine would also be essential, as he wouldn't have a full crew.

With each stroke of the oars, Serrano marvelled at the phosphorescence dancing in the seawater around their dinghy. There were few places in the world he thought that could rival his experience of the West of Scotland. It was so different from the frenetic life that he led back home. He regretted very much that for him this visit was more than likely to be his last.

He had paid the representatives of the charter company handsomely for their services, and to compensate for the fact that despite his claimed experience, he was unable to produce documentation to evidence any valid sailing qualification. His largesse also meant that if officialdom came calling, he hoped they would be entirely discreet about their clients' whereabouts.

Normally those seeking a "bareboat charter" (a phrase which, despite his reasonable English, Serrano at first misinterpreted) are expected to leave details of their proposed itinerary, but a vague description of "west coast cruising" was all that the Colombians gave. Although the yacht was Category 2 registered, which meant a range of 60 miles from any safe haven, this would not constrain them for the west coast passage that they had in mind.

Jose Maria usually had hired hands to do the sailing for him but on this occasion and for reasons that would become only too clear in due course, the couple were on their own.

When they arrived at the mooring, they unloaded the tender and made it fast for the night. Luz Marina, who normally did not accompany her husband on his sailing trips and was something of a reluctant participant, chipped one of her long fingernails in the process and was not pleased.

An early bed was called for. They would be up early the next morning to take advantage of the tide, and to slip away quietly from their mooring without attracting any attention.

-Chapter Eighty-

The couple awoke at daybreak to the sound of halyards flapping against the metal masts of nearby boats. The inshore weather forecast confirmed what they already knew. The wind was freshening from the west.

Luz Marina was first to have her shower while Serrano slipped a pair of jeans on and busied himself on deck. He was too preoccupied with his problems at home and in the UK to even think of sharing the shower, which in any event was somewhat smaller than those they were accustomed to.

Within half an hour they had hoisted the mainsail and had left Largs Bay, watched carefully and photographed dutifully from the shore by DI Turner. The officer's personal preference would have been to arrest Jose Maria before the pair embarked, but DS Ramsay's clear instruction for some time now had been to covertly observe only. There were, apparently, reasons known only to the most senior officers why the drugs baron was still being allowed to remain at large.

Turner had his own suspicions.

"Was there a clandestine rendezvous planned for some remote location? Was Serrano planning to meet someone with yet another shipment from abroad?

Surely he would not be so brazen as to collect a delivery himself when he must know that he is under surveillance? - After all, a fairly large yacht was their vessel of choice when a smaller one would have been more than adequate for two people."

Turner was missing something.

Perhaps if the DI had understood a little more of the philosophy of Jose Maria, he would have realised that he no longer needed to get his hands dirty. There was no possibility whatsoever of him coming anywhere near the merchandise. He paid others to do his dirty work, as he himself had done in his now distant past.

And Luz Marina emphatically did not like small boats, hence the Bavaria being chartered to keep her satisfied.

Even on the water, Serrano was still communicating regularly with his empire, using every trick in the book to avoid detection. He was good at that, and quite cocksure of himself, but even although his elaborate data encryption was up to the standards of many a small country, Ramsay believed that eventually it would prove no match for Britain's finest.

The experts had advised that they needed only another few days to verify some of the translations into English, and crosscheck the mass of evidence that had been gathered against the Colombians. The way would then be clear, certainly as far as the UK was concerned, for the enforcement agencies to carry out joint raids.

These would ensure the concurrent arrests not only of Jose Maria, but also of his Cartel associates. The exact timings would not be announced in advance and would depend upon certain international operations that should conclude within the next seven days.

It was vitally important in the meantime that Serrano did not have his or the Cartel's suspicions aroused, and have the opportunity to alert others; even if this were simply as a result of someone in the UK or Colombia missing their regular phone or email instructions from him.

DI Turner noted that his surveillance of the Colombians would therefore be very low key from that point on.

-Chapter Eighty One-

Luz Marina sat across the large well laid out cockpit from her husband, looking more like a fashion model about to go on a photo-shoot than a Captain's mate. She studied him intently.

She thought that he looked every bit the consummate skipper, totally in command of the yacht and making good headway across the Firth. The wind was now on the beam so the ride was quite comfortable, despite the swell.

Luz Marina was not accustomed to manoeuvres such as beating into the wind with the yacht close-hauled. Leaning over so far made her feel insecure. It was a pleasant change, therefore, to be able to relax a little. The sun had even made a few appearances from between the fast moving clouds that were scurrying across the sky.

"If day to day life," she thought, "were more like this I might be able to tolerate my husband and his idiosyncrasies."

What she could never condone was his jealous nature and, above all, his cruelty to his fellow man.

In a sad sort of way, she had begun to see parallels between him and Kim Jong-un, the North Korean dictator who she had read was not averse to killing anyone who got in his way, even including members of his own family. At least Jose Maria had a normal haircut.

The age difference between the couple of some 15 years was something that she did not like to think about. When they were alone together such as just now, it did not matter at all. She still found him handsome and somewhat distinguished looking, even with his hair that was now greying from the edges.

His power and authority seemed like an aphrodisiac.

"Who needed the expensive oysters that her husband had flown in regularly from a bay near Arcachon?"

She did not, however, lust after him in the way she had when he had first held her in his strong arms and swept her off her feet.

The age gap mattered only when she was in male company closer to her own age, and this made her afraid for their future together. Then she had learned to lose herself in her dreams, remembering her carefree life in the theatre, especially with one of the penniless male dancers named Pedro who had been her first and only real love, and even the young air steward with whom she had made intense and knowing eye contact on the flight over from Bogota.

Gradually she was losing touch with her former friends, and even to some extent, her family. Her husband was responsible for this, and she hated him for it.

"Can someone both love and hate the same person at the same time?"

Her answer was an unequivocal "yes", but she had always had slight schizophrenic tendencies. These had become more noticeable lately, and she put this down to an unfortunate side effect of occasional personal consumption of her husband's product. Either that, or she had simply had enough of Serrano and his esoteric way of earning his living. Or maybe he was simply becoming boring and more predictable in bed?

She had certainly reached beyond the poverty of her former life. She always lived for the moment as she was doing now, but she could never see this bringing the real long-term happiness and fulfilment that she so craved.

Soon they reached their anchorage for the night.

Being a dutiful wife, she responded immediately to Jose Maria's command to operate the electric anchor winch. She then climbed into the comfortable double cabin that they shared. It was situated forward of the main saloon.

She was wearing expensive French perfume and the very latest short nightie in dusky pink from her favourite line of designer lingerie, which she had bought specially in anticipation of this trip. The Faire Frou Frou brand is not the most expensive in the world, but is probably in the top ten. As its name suggests it is for those who like to show off, and she certainly could.

The skipper joined her about three hours later after completing some pressing work on his laptop at the chart table. He smiled briefly in recognition of the vision that met his eyes.

"She did try very hard for him."

By this time the gentle movement of the waves had lulled Luz Marina to sleep and she was dreaming of having fun with her young and handsome Pedro. It was just as well that she did not talk in her sleep.

Jose Maria uncharacteristically chose not to wake her.

Clearly his stress was beginning to show.

-Chapter Eighty Two-

Iain Ramsay by now had finalised his joint case papers and passed them up the line. Needless to say this was a great relief to Mrs Ramsay, who ever since the episode with the fish finger in Troon, was a firm convert to the doctrine of early retirement. She never missed an opportunity to preach this particular Gospel to her husband and from his pained expression whenever the subject was brought up, it looked as if even he might soon be converted.

The DS had already built up quite a reputation in police circles and there was nothing quite like quitting at the top of one's game.

"Who knows", she suggested "he might even write a book on his exploits?"

All feedback from SOCA and other colleagues, on the reports that he had filed, had been positive. Some crucial gaps in the overall evidence had eventually been closed by the painstaking and professional work done in Scotland, and this was considered sufficient to identify and charge those running the Colombian route.

Ramsay's team tactics however unorthodox and difficult in practice, of patient surveillance rather than making immediate arrests, had clearly paid off. They had given their targets sufficient rope to hang themselves. There was even talk of using elements of Operations Duck Bay and Viking as case studies at the Tulliallan National Police Training College.

Data transmissions to and from Serrano's laptop had not proved as secure as he believed. Interceptions from the yacht that related to the laundering of the Cartel's money were sufficient to ensure that actions would eventually be possible to seize major funds under the Proceeds of Crime Act, or its international equivalents.

Jose Maria remained happily oblivious to the fact that his various enterprises had been compromised to this degree.

His immediate concerns had related to the rumours of insubordination in the ranks, which had emanated from Bogota after the loss of the Miraflor.

However, after reading again Paulo's response to his latest email, which was brief and to the point, he managed to convince himself that this imminent threat to his authority had been dealt with in the customary manner.

He could trust Paulo as much as anyone.

After all they were both boys from Bucaramanga!

-Chapter Eighty Three-

To all the world the couple on the Bavaria were typical West Coast tourists, taking in the sights and sounds of some of the finest cruising grounds the world has to offer.

They had sailed northwest from Largs, leaving the Firth of Clyde and the verdant Isle of Bute with its Victorian spa town capital, Rothesay, behind them on the port side.

En route something surreal happened. They found themselves spending quality time not only with each other but also with a basking shark, the second largest fish in the world, when it came alongside. It seemed reluctant to leave, even rubbing itself against the hull of their boat, but eventually they had to sail on and leave it behind.

They were astonished that it was almost 30 feet in length. It was greyish brown with mottled skin. Luz

Marina having seen the size of its mouth at close quarters only relaxed when she learned that it was a docile creature, which spent its whole life swallowing only plankton; the same tiny plankton that earlier that day had been responsible for the amazing phosphorescence they had seen sparkling in the seawater off Largs.

On the mooring for the night at Colintraive, they had done a spot of fishing with the gear provided on board, and surprised themselves by quickly catching a couple of mackerel for their evening meal. They nearly didn't eat when a squabble of seagulls spotted their catch and decided to compete with them for it, but the fish eventually did end up in their frying pan. It was a memorable evening, even if the noisy birds only left when the last morsel of mackerel had gone.

Next morning in beautiful sunshine and with barely a ripple on the crystal clear water they used the engine for the first time, making their leisurely way through the magnificent narrows of the Kyles of Bute, around Ardlamont Point and across to the picturesque fishing village of Tarbert on Loch Fyne.

Tarbert harbour was surprisingly busy and the quayside resplendent in festive bunting. The fleet was in town, as well as several dozen yachts from Northern Ireland whose owners were socialising loudly on deck. There was the smell of barbecued fish in the air, the sound of a fiddle playing, and much merriment.

The visitors had no option but to moor alongside one of these boats, but declined an invitation to come on deck and join the party. The less people knew about them and their business, the better.

They even failed to surface from below deck when one of the high-spirited youngsters at the party, fuelled by vodka, thought that she would have some fun by setting off one of the emergency flares from the stern of her neighbour's yacht. Needless to say, the neighbour was not pleased.

When he heard the bang Jose Maria's immediate reaction was to reach under the sink for his handgun. He was relieved when he realised that the commotion was only as a result of a silly prank.

This meant further unwanted excitement for the Colombians about half an hour later when blue lights from a police car started flashing on the nearby pier. They began to imagine the worst, but it was a false alarm again.

The arrival of the police was an unfortunate consequence of the young lady's flare, blown by the evening breeze, parachuting down into a field beyond the historic Tarbert Castle where the pyrotechnic had quickly set fire to the undergrowth. It looked dramatic enough on the skyline from a harbour viewpoint, but must have been frightening for those residents of the village whose homes were at risk until the fire brigade had sorted things out. Some of the properties were on private water supplies drawn from further up the hill, and the poor flow of water to hoses complicated matters for the fire brigade.

Serrano was sitting at the boat's chart table. At this point in their journey, he required to consult his chart, and over a coffee he was carefully considering a couple of options for the morning:

"Should he continue up Loch Fyne to Ardrishaig and the Crinan Canal, or should he take the longer route around the exposed Mull of Kintyre, then north between Islay and Gigha and so into the Sound of Jura?"

Luz Marina had seen the week afloat as a useful and rare opportunity to get to know her husband better because, strange to relate, she had never really spent any length of quality time with him on her own. She sensed, however, that he was still totally preoccupied with his business problems at home and abroad.

For days he had avoided any kind of intimacy.

His eventual choice of taking the long way around the Kintyre Peninsula even although the wind was again freshening strongly from the Atlantic would certainly not be conducive to their having a quiet time together.

From Luz Marina's point of view, she much would have preferred a gentle sail up Loch Fyne followed by the quiet nine miles passage through the 15 locks of the wonderful Crinan Canal, built in 1801 and used by no less a person than Queen Victoria for her holidays in 1847.

She could picture the Royal Barge being drawn in those days by four horses, two of which were ridden by fit-looking postillions in Royal livery. She had read about this in some tourist literature, which helpfully was reproduced for her in Spanish.

Jose Maria, however, had his own agenda. No matter how quaint or picturesque, the narrow confines of the Crinan Canal were not to his liking.

It was far from ideal for someone who does not wish to broadcast his whereabouts. To transit the canal would be equivalent to taking out a full-page spread in the local Oban Times or Argyllshire Advertiser announcing their location. Even worse, they could be ambushed quite easily in any of the sea locks and would have nowhere to hide. He noted also that there was really only one single-track road along the canal from Cairnbaan towards Crinan, a road that could quite easily be blocked by police.

Although he had not yet told his wife, his plan was therefore to sail non-stop up the west of Kintyre and thence into the Firth of Lorn, where he had an important rendezvous at a secret island location.

-Chapter Eighty Four-

The Isle of Mull is the second largest island of the Inner Hebrides.

It was well after midnight when the Bavaria rounded the headland. They saw the formidable dark silhouette of the 13th century Duart Castle (famous as a film location as well as the seat of the Clan MacLean) on their port side, and proceeded up the Sound of Mull. She found sanctuary in the relative shelter of Tobermory Bay, as so many vessels including some from the Spanish Armada way back in 1588, had done before her.

The passage up from Tarbert, Loch Fyne had been a bit of a nightmare, with wind against tide and waves well in excess of six feet. Even the extremely rare sight earlier in the evening of what she thought was a white-tailed sea eagle in flight against a crimson sky had done nothing to calm Luz Marina. Her husband had rubbished her identification of what they both had seen, but with her expensive camera's long lens she had managed to get quite a good photograph of it for future clarification. Nevertheless she still wanted to go home.

Serrano wanted to go home too. That was why they left the yacht anchored in the Bay the next morning, rowed ashore to the pier and were met on the quayside by one of the Cartel's operatives. His job was to drive them the short distance to the Glenforsa Hotel on the north coast for breakfast. Luz Marina began to suspect that something was afoot.

The hotel happens to be somewhat unique in that there is an unlicensed grass airfield adjacent to the hotel.

The runway is a grass strip 780m by 28m with a slight slope down to the sea. The Royal Engineers built it in this remote location to facilitate fixed-wing air ambulance flights to and from the local Salen Hospital. The better-equipped Oban hospital was only some 15 minutes away by air.

Hazards for pilots at Glenforsa include high local terrain, turbulence with approaches on strong southerly winds, livestock on the runway from October to April, and the danger of geese at almost any time. Despite its limitations, however, the airfield regularly welcomes light aircraft and has an excellent safety record.

One notable exception, which the Serranos did not know about, was the well-documented Mull Air Mystery. This involved a former Spitfire pilot named Peter Gibbs who took off from Glenforsa on the evening of 24th December 1975. Months later his body was found 400 feet up a hillside with no sign of external injuries, but it wasn't until 1986 that a local diver found his plane at least 300 yards offshore. There had, however, been no evidence of seawater or marine life on the pilot's body. So this was a real mystery and no satisfactory explanation has ever been found to account for the tragedy.

Over a hearty breakfast at the Glenforsa hotel Jose Maria had the difficult job of explaining to Luz Marina that a Cessna would be arriving soon to pick him up and fly him away from the clutches of the Scottish police.

He could not afford to hang about as the net was closing in on him. He had heard this from Paulo who had made the arrangements. The flight turnaround would be 10 minutes at most.

Jose Maria was sorry for the apparent deception but apart from the pilot the plane only had one seat. The surly driver who had brought them from Tobermory would therefore look after his wife, driving her to another location where after a few days she would leave by fishing boat under cover of darkness and make her way to Ireland. His Irish representative would contact her whenever her boat made landfall.

There she would be suitably disguised and fly out on a tourist charter under an assumed name and on a false passport.

He dismissed her protestations with a shrug of the shoulders, and coldly said

"It is better for us to travel independently anyway."

From Luz Marina's perspective, this was the final straw. South American women are known to be feisty, but she broke the mould.

"How dare he abandon her like this?"

She was left with a substantial wad of sterling, but otherwise only the sailing clothes that she stood up in. Her other belongings, including her favourite pieces of jewellery that she might never be able to retrieve and her Jimmy Shoo sandals, were left behind in the yacht. She was now expected to behave like a fugitive and use false papers when her only crime had been to marry the wrong man.

Her world was falling apart, just as her mother had predicted!

Nevertheless she had her stage training and experience to fall back on now. Like the professional actor she had been, she would assume the character of whoever was necessary in order to get safely back to Bogota, by whatever circuitous route her selfish, bullying and inconsiderate husband had planned for her.

"What would she do now?"

She did not know. She felt that her husband was becoming more and more distant, and utterly unreasonable. His actions were clearly premeditated despite his protestations and feeble apologies to her. The Scottish trip had been a revelation.

"This couldn't go on!"

She didn't even stay at Glenforsa to wave her husband off. She told him quite forcefully that she didn't care if she never saw him again. She then turned her toned back on him before he even had time to reply. She made purposefully for the door without so much as a backwards glance.

It was painfully clear that they were no longer the couple that had flown out in luxury on the BA Flight from Aeropuerto Eldorado.

-Chapter Eighty Five-

Detective Inspector Turner arrived at the airstrip on Mull just in time to see Serrano's small Cessna disappear over the horizon.

He was also there having a leisurely lunch of local seafood spaghetti washed down by a quite acceptable chilled Sauvignon Blanc, when he received the message that a fleet of trawlers in the middle of the Irish Sea had seen a small plane explode spectacularly above their heads. It fell in many pieces to the water below.

The trawlermen were now doing another kind of fishing.

-Chapter Eighty Six-

Still angry with Jose Maria and blissfully unaware of his demise, his beautiful and now extremely wealthy young widow was soon en route to a small and unremarkable bed and breakfast establishment in the sleepy town of Oban.

In stark contrast, the lounge bar of the Casa Grande Cabacera Hotel in the commercial area of Bucaramanga was buzzing. - Three men sat cosily in a corner celebrating with the finest vintage champagne.

They weren't there in Bucaramanga to soak up the history or culture of Colombia's City of Parks that had been founded in 1622; or like the many tourists booked into the hotel, to spend time leisurely exploring the north-eastern foothills of the Andes. They had their own agenda.

The first amigo was the late Jose Maria's ever-attentive Paulo, the second Paulo's own newly-appointed minder from his immediate family, and the third a bare-chested and dark skinned male dancer who until very recently had been treading the boards of the Teatro Cristobal Colon in Bogota.

El final.

Hasta el proximo encuentro…

About the Author

Dawson Lamont is a Scottish Chartered Accountant who after a career in Local Government Finance has turned his attention from creative accounting to creative writing.

While at school in Ayrshire many years ago, he was encouraged to write by his English teacher, none other than William McIlvanney, the father of Tartan Noir.

Now Dawson is based in Inverness where he lives happily with his wife Eleanor. They have two grown-up children Stephanie and Tristan, a son-in-law Jonathan, and two adorable granddaughters Amelie and Juliette.

Cover Design is by Jonathan Morley.